Sword
Of the
Matchmaker
Winds of Change

Copyright © 2017
Sword of the Matchmaker
Winds of Change
Written by Debbie Lynne Costello
Published by: Wakefield Press
Cover design: The Killion Group, Inc
www.TheKillionGroupInc.com

ISBN- 13:978-0-9861820-7-5
ISBN- 10: 0-9861820-7-9

Glossary

Anon – soon, shortly

Bailey – an open area inside the castle complex, the bailey contained the domestic and other necessary buildings of castle life. An inner bailey lay in an area inside the main castle and its safety, while the outer bailey was outside the main castle defenses, making it more vulnerable should there be an attack.

Chemise – long loose undergarment for women.

Courtly Love – a time when many marriages were not for love, courtly love followed rules and allowed a man and a woman to outwardly show their affections for each other.

Dais – raised platform.

Demesne – part of the estate of the lord of the manor for his own use and support and often sub-leased.

Destrier – warhorse.

Dinna – did not

Flagstone – a flat stone used for flooring at this time period.

Fortnight – 14 days.

Garth – small enclosed or fenced area.

Guid – good

Great Hall – multi-purpose room where meals were taken, guests received, business conducted, and even used as sleeping quarters when needed.

Keep – fortified tower in the castle.

Kirtle – a piece of clothing typically worn over a chemise and under the outer garment gown/surcoat.

Ladily – word used in place of ladylike in 14th century.

Mews – housing for falcons and hawks.

Plait – a braid or plait of hair.

Portcullis – a strong heavy gate sliding up and down. This is lowered to block a gateway to a fortress.

Prithee – pray thee

Sennight – 7 days.

Solar – private sitting room often found above

and used by family and close friends. Solars could be connected to bedrooms.

Squire – shield-bearer or armor-bearer to the knight. Squires are promoted from the rank of page at about the age of thirteen or fourteen, they were then trained further in knightly pursuits. The squire was a candidate for the honor of knighthood, and learned from the knight he was squire to by performing any tasks that the knight might require.

Tae – to

Trencher – trenchers were used to serve and eat food, much like modern day plates. Stale loaves of bread (or stale crusts of bread) were used to soak up food and eat it. Leftover pieces of trenchers were often given to the dogs or distributed to the poor as alms.

Tunic – the medieval equivalent of a shirt. A tunic was usually longer and looser than a modern shirt.

Wimple – headdress
Yer – your

Chapter 1

Cumberland, England, 1399

Penelope peered through the woodland at the fortress with its thick walls, battlements and towers. What an intimidating sight in comparison to the small village from which she hailed. Even clad in breeches with a knife on her leg, a sword on her back and a bow slung over her shoulder, Penelope didn't feel like the warrior she'd grown up to be.

At age twenty-five, she'd spent the last twelve years fighting battles and protecting those who needed protection. But being truly alone for the first time in her life and on English soil suddenly made her feel small and insignificant.

She parted the tall green stems of the bishop's lace with her hands and stepped from the shadows of the forest into the sunlight, never taking her eyes off her destination—Hawkwood.

As if the ground had conjured up soldiers, she was surrounded by men on horseback. Reaching for the hilt of her sword which protruded over her shoulder, the clanging of blades removed from their sheaths gave her pause. She let her hand return to her side, pulled back her shoulders to show her full height and lifted her chin as her eyes searched for the leader.

She didn't need to search long. The man she needed to address held himself as only a knight of position would.

Ignoring the swords pointed her way, she stepped toward the leader. "Me name is Penelope Beatty and I have come tae speak with Hamon Godfrey."

He raised a brow but didn't say a word. The way the other men suddenly shifted their gaze from her to him caused a knot to form in her gut. Certainly this couldn't be Hamon. He was much too young…wasn't he? She'd never asked her father the age of the man he'd saved. She'd always assumed Hamon was her father's age and for some reason seeking a man her father's age comforted her.

"I have come tae call in a favor that is owed." Couldn't these men speak?

The corner of the man's mouth twitched in what she could only assume was amusement.

"I wish you tae take me tae Hamon Godfrey." In her most authoritative voice added, "Now."

"Hamon Godfrey owes you a favor?" The black- haired leader spoke from his mount. "I venture to say that you could not have been much more than a babe when…you last saw him. I assure you Hamon has not stepped off English soil since you were a bairn."

The other men chuckled at his response and he

grinned. That made the blood in her veins as hot as the red coals she wished to heap upon his head. "I assure you, Sir Hamon will see me, perhaps even welcome me." She'd thrown that last bit in for good measure. She had no idea if the man would be happy to repay his debt.

"I am sure Hamon would be delighted to give you a proper welcome."

Hope arose within her. "Then you'll take me tae him?"

He cocked his head and shrugged. "As you wish."

Leaning down over the side of his destrier, he stretched out his arm and gave her his hand. No sooner had she clasped hold of his hand that he pulled her onto his horse in front of him. She'd thought to swing up behind but he'd been faster than her.

"You dress like a man." His warm breath pushed past her ear.

She stiffened. "And I fight better than most."

The rumble of hearty laughter in his chest angered her. She could only imagine he was a typical Englishman. A reason why she shouldn't have come.

"You are a long way from home." He urged his mount forward and the other men followed.

Everything the man said rubbed her wrong. How did he know where she was from and why did he find so much mirth out of her being there? "Am I?"

"Hmmm. I would say the highlands of Scotland.

'Tis a long way for one wee lass to come."

"'Tis nothing wee aboot me. Ye would no' question a man should he have come this far."

"'Tis true. But I also would not be taking him to see Hamon. Rather, I would be escorting him to see Lord Royce and questioning why he was here."

Hearing him repeat that he was taking her to Hamon gave her some comfort. "I would imagine I will need tae speak with your laird, also. After I speak with Hamon, that is."

"Aye, you will need to speak with Royce."

"Do you have a name?" She'd waited long enough for the man to introduce himself. She'd like to know with whom she rode and spoke.

"Aye, I do."

She could hear the humor return to his voice. She stiffened. That was the last question she would ask the man. He had no honor. Heaven help her if she had to remain in England with these dolts.

"'Tis Sir Thomas, at your service." Another chuckle.

She loathed the man. Though she wanted to tell him she did not need his service, she precisely did. Without him taking her to Hamon she would have no way of finding him.

Instead of heading on up to the castle, they had veered off in the direction of the village. Meeting with Hamon could not happen soon enough for her. Sir Thomas wasn't the first man who didn't take her seriously as a soldier. She'd been laughed at, been the object of many jokes, and been shunned by as many women as men, but this was her calling and she'd not make an excuse for it. Though she was oft' the object of sport, none would deny her talent.

As they drew close to the village they rode along a cemetery on the left. The men behind her slowed until she could no longer hear the horse's hooves hitting the ground. She turned around out of curiosity and found they had stopped. Sir Thomas must have given them a signal that she'd missed. Not surprising since she rode in front of the man.

From where she sat, Penelope could see that many of the cottages were rather new. Her gaze swept over the outer row of wattle and daub homes with thatch roofs. She couldn't help but wonder if Hamon owned one of the larger homes in the village. For some reason, she'd envisioned him an important man at Hawkwood.

But then when her father had told her about Hamon, the grief inside her was so great, she barely heard what he'd said, causing him to repeat himself even as he lay on his deathbed. Her father's journey to death remained the hardest thing she'd ever faced. He was her crusader, her teacher, her protector. She'd learned everything she knew from him. She was the son he'd never had and she'd made a point not to let him down.

She supposed that was why he took the sacred cross from his pocket and wrapped it in her hand— the cross that many felt gave the owner the right to be leader of a clan and would bring blessings to the holder. Unless that owner was a woman. She'd sewn the cross into the crown of her hat to keep it safe. She touched the hiding place at her forehead to remind herself of her father's blessing, and basked for a moment in the confidence it gave her.

With her thoughts drawn back home to Scotland and with her Da, she'd not realized they'd stopped beside a grave. Heavens! If she'd have been so dull-witted on her journey to Hawkwood, she'd never have survived the trip.

Sir Thomas dismounted and reached up for her. She'd never had a man help her off a horse and she'd not start now. "'Tis quite capable I am of getting off a mount." She said the words as she ignored his hands and swung to the ground.

"As you wish." The one corner of Sir Thomas's mouth pulled back into what was surely mirth.

She'd only have to put up with the man a few more minutes and she would never have to deal with him again. "Does Hamon care for the grounds here?" She glanced around searching for the older man sought, but saw no one.

"Nay, Hamon does not."

She shoved her fists on her hips. "Then why have we stopped here?"

"You wished to see Hamon. And here he is." Sir Thomas opened one arm wide and extended it toward the closest grave.

"Do...do you mean tae tell me that Ha...Hamon is dead?"

Chapter 2

Thomas hesitated. Why hadn't he just told the woman that his father was dead? It wasn't like him to play games with people. He usually got right to the point. He supposed it was despite her garb or perhaps because of it, she made him smile.

"Aye, he is dead. Been dead for nigh onto fifteen years."

The woman warrior's shoulders dropped and for just a trice, he'd thought her legs would give out from beneath her. He eyed her cautiously. What kind of favor could his father owe this lass? She'd been not much more than a child when his father had passed. Why, at twenty, he'd barely been a man himself.

"Then," she paused and swallowed. "I have come all this way for nothing."

Meeting up with his father had been much more important to her than he'd thought or he'd not have brought her to his father's grave.

"Perhaps I can help you." He owed her that for

tormenting her.

"Nay, 'twas Hamon who owed my father his life. 'Tis no' your debt tae pay."

Thomas's brow shot up. Her father saved his father? He'd not heard that story. But it did help his case. "Ah, but then perhaps it is my debt to pay. Let me introduce myself—"

"Nay." Her denial was quick and cut him off. "I'll no' be indebted tae an Englishman."

Thomas held back a smile. So, the lass didn't like the English. "As I was saying, let me introduce myself. I am Sir Thomas Godfrey. Son of Hamon Godfrey." He gave a slight bow.

"Hamon's son?"

"Aye, I am his eldest son."

"Then you ken the debt your father owed my father, Niall Beatty?"

Thomas hesitated. He hated to tell her he'd not heard any such story. "I did not. But I was away much of my younger years as a page and a squire."

"I see." She tipped her head to the side. "But you believe me?"

Thomas shrugged. "I have no reason not to."

This tall woman before him stood proud with her long red hair pulled away from her face and trailing down her back. Despite her male fighting garb, she was beautiful. Thomas shook himself out of his stupor. He didn't need or want a woman. He'd done quite well without one to this point. There was no reason to tempt fate. Even as beautiful as she was, the last kind of woman he wanted was one who wanted to fight on the battlefield. If he wanted a woman, he wanted one who was soft and sweet. He spent enough time with battle- hardened men.

"Would you like tae ken the story?"

He hoped it would make her feel better telling why his father owed her a debt so he nodded. "Aye."

"'Twas when your da and my da were young. My mither grieved so over the loss of her betrothed, my da, that her parents sent her tae visit her grandmither here in England. While here she met Hamon. He fell in love with her and wanted tae marry her, but she would no' give him an answer until she spoke with her parents. So Hamon started the journey tae bring my mither back tae her clan, but on the way my da intercepted them. My da had been wounded in a clan battle and almost died as their prisoner. But he escaped and made it home only tae learn my mither had gone tae England. He was on his way tae bring her home when he came upon your da with her. Your da was furious and challenged my da tae a duel but before they could begin, they were come upon by brigands. They had dispatched all but one when the brigand raised his blade from behind your da. My da managed tae get there just in time tae stop the blade from coming down and killing him.

"I would guess that is when your da came tae his senses and asked my mither which man she wished tae marry. When she chose my da, Hamon withdrew his request for a duel and told my da if he could ever repay the debt, my mither knew where tae find him."

Niall sounded like a very good storyteller to Thomas. But he wouldn't tell Penelope that. He did faintly remember hearing his father had braved the Scottish hills for a lass. But he was young and had not been in on the conversation so didn't remember much about it.

"If my father owed you a debt, as the eldest son it is now my debt to pay." Thomas spoke with all the conviction he could muster. This lady champion of others looked as if she had not much fight left in her despite her attempt to appear the opposite.

The top of her head reached nearly to his nose and he was no small man. He had expected to see her tip her head slightly to look him in the eyes, but instead her gaze fell to the ground. "'Tis ashamed I am tae ask."

Thomas's heart cinched. This beautiful lass before him was very much a woman no matter how much she wanted to play the knight.

"You were going to ask my father." Thomas reminded her.

The mid-day sun hung high in the sky. A light breeze gave relief from the early summer's heat and tousled her hair as she lifted her head. She pushed her hair away from her face with the back of her hand as she lifted her gaze to his. Brown eyes that held the weight of the world stared back at him. She glanced over her shoulder, as if to see where his men were and if they were within earshot.

"But he owed a debt. You dinna. 'Tis different. A warrior likes tae pay their debts." She blinked and her long lashes brushed her skin.

Everything about the woman contradicted who she was. He turned away, fixing his gaze on a patch of purple and white flowers beyond the cemetery. Never had a woman intrigued him so. He turned back to her and brushed away the hiccup of his heart. Never would he be interested in a woman combatant. "And a knight likes to pay his father's debts." He countered. "Prithee, tell me how I may be of service to you, lass."

She stole another quick glance over her shoulder. What could be so bad that the lass could not get the words out?

"Would it be easier if you started from the beginning?"

A hint of a smile played on her lips and the wrinkles in her forehead faded. "Aye, 'twould."

"Then let us start there." He took her arm and guided her over to a bench he'd made at his lord's wife's request. Brithwin always thought of others and wanted a place for people to sit if they desired to be near their loved ones. "Now, you will start from the beginning."

She nodded, and he almost gave a sigh of relief. "You must understand, my da's clan is a small clan. The MacAlisters, a neighboring clan, accused one of our men of thieving and we knew it no' tae be so. My da would no' back down. 'Twas aboot honor. Our clans battled but we were smaller, we dinna stand a chance. Most of my people were killed." She turned away and gazed toward the same wildflowers he had only moments earlier.

Thomas drew his brow down. "You chose honor over the lives of your clan?" He wouldn't say it, but allowing women and children to die, either by the sword or starvation was not honorable in his sight.

Whether she was so lost in her thoughts and didn't hear or if she chose to ignore him, he didn't know. But she continued as if he'd not spoken a word.

"My father lay mortally wounded and as he die, he sent me tae Hamon Godfrey. But I dinna wish tae come crawling tae the English."

She said the words with so much venom, Thomas expected her to glare at him. But her expression didn't change.

"Instead, I stayed and helped the few people who had survived the massacre. But as the days went on I overcame my grief of losing my da and grew angry. I sought revenge on the MacAlisters. Eventually, I was captured and sentenced tae die. I escaped and have spent the last three months eluding my captors."

Thomas waited to see if she had more to say. But she continued to stare off as if reliving what she'd been through.

"You wish me to help you seek revenge on your enemy?" By the rood! What mess had he gotten himself into? There was enough tension on the border now. Royce himself had to squash down an uprising right before he and Brithwin married. Going up into Scotland to seek revenge on a clan he had no issue with would only cause more problems for all the borderlands.

Perhaps he could reason with her. It wasn't as if he had his own army. He was Royce's master-at-arms. He couldn't just take knights away from Hawkwood and go fight a warrior woman's battle.

"Nay, 'tis no' your battle tae fight."

Thomas observed the lass while his mind raced for what she could possibly want from his father if not retribution. "If not vengeance, then what is this favor you wish to ask of me?"

She drew in a deep breath and let it out before turning to him. Her long lashes fluttered and for a second he didn't think she would look him in the eye when she told him. But to her credit, she did.

"I need sanctuary. The only thing I can offer you in return is my services as a warrior."

Thomas nearly choked. That would be the day when he would allow a woman to serve beside his knights.

Before he knew what she was about, the woman was off the bench and fell to her knees before him. "I swear to you my loyalty."

"Pleased I am, lass. But you need not—"

Thomas had not gotten all the words out of his mouth when she rose up off her knees, bent over him and kissed both cheeks.

She straightened before him. "As you have my loyalty so also you have my alliance. I am seasoned in the art of battle, I offer to you my services."

Remaining seated, Thomas heard the chuckles from the men when she'd fallen to her knees. The kiss to each cheek they did not let pass by so easily. They began throwing comments his way about him needing lessons on how to handle a woman, and offering their services. He chose to ignore them.

"That will not be necessary, lass. No payment will be required, I assure you. 'Tis a debt being paid." He knew his lady, and Brithwin would be beside herself with joy to have another lady in the castle. "Come. I will introduce you to Lord Royce and Lady Brithwin."

Penelope had risen from her knees with such grace, Thomas had a hard time believing this woman though dressed in a man's vestments was a fighter. For the only thing that gave hint to that was her clothing.

And he was not the only one who had noticed. His men's comments were proof they saw the same thing. He was not happy with them now. And when he finished working them on the field they would know it and not be likely to forget any time soon

"Wife!" He called to his horse and the animal moved to stand in front of them.

Penelope turned to him. "Wife?"

"Aye 'tis the only one I will have."

Penelope swung up onto the horse as if the animal were no taller than Brithwin's Wolfhound. Thomas had all he could do to not gawk at the lass. Truly it was as if she were two people in one body.

He swung up behind her and spurred Wife toward Hawkwood. Something in him stirred and he suddenly knew that nothing would be the same after today. He could picture in his mind's eye Brithwin championing the lass and wanting her to be a part of security at the castle. Lord have mercy, he hoped he was wrong, but when Brithwin got something into her head she usually ended up having her way.

Chapter 3

Penelope kept her back straight as she rode into Hawkwood, vexed with Sir Thomas at his abrupt refusal of aid from her. She even had to question if he'd accepted her loyalty to him. It wasn't many times in her life that she'd sworn her loyalty and alliance to someone with her clan's sacred custom of kneeling before them and kissing them. It angered her that he'd not realized the honor she'd just bestowed on him.

And of course, he wouldn't wish for her help because no man believed a woman could do any job as well as he. Especially a man who would name a horse "Wife". The man was as uncouth as they come. Did he compare a wife to the likes of an animal or worse, did he consider her chattel just as a horse?

The two passed through the open portcullis and into the inner bailey. It was a fine castle. Her gaze swept up to the curtain wall where knights patrolled—it would be a safe haven.

Acrid smoke from the smith shop blew their way. She glanced over as the blacksmith's hammer came down on a piece of metal sending a crash into the air. A large fire burned beside the man as he pounded on the glowing iron.

Childlike laughter drew her attention away. She searched out the joyful lad to find him watching the falconer as he tossed meat and sent a hawk for its meal.

A sense of peace settled over Penelope. Hawkwood was a fine keep. Her father indeed was wise to send her here.

Sir Thomas reined in his mount near a garth with a garden of flowers the colors of a rainbow. He swung down and raised his hands to help her. She refrained from rolling her eyes heavenward and slid off the horse. Could the man not see that she was quite capable to mount and dismount the beast?

He ignored her slight and gave a small bow as he swept out his arm for her to go ahead of him. "We will most likely find milady in her garden." As if thinking better of things he stopped her. "But before we do, I think it best to leave your weapons here."

She gave a nod and handed him her bow, knife, and sword before she strode past him. She imagined the Lady Brithwin fluttered around her flowers, bending and smelling them all. She let out a sigh, preparing herself for the introduction. She would learn to tolerate the woman.

But the woman she envisioned was not the woman they stopped near. Nay, the woman Sir

Thomas now looked down upon was on her hands and knees covered in dirt, pulling out weeds.

"Milady." Thomas spoke to the woman.

Milady? Penelope nearly made a most unladylike sound.

Lady Brithwin looked up and Penelope stared into eyes as blue as the summer sky. The woman smiled and stood. "Thomas, I see you have brought company."

"Aye, milady. This is Penelope Beatty, from the highlands of Scotland."

Brithwin's smile grew. "'Tis good of you to come.

We do not get nearly enough visitors."

"Thank you, milady." Penelope gave a nod of her head. "'Tis guid indeed tae be here."

"Penelope needs a place to stay. 'Twould be a personal favor to me milady, if you would consider it." Sir Thomas spoke with formality but Penelope had a feeling that the two were much closer than he let on.

"Of course, Thomas," she placed a soiled hand on his sleeve then seemed to think better of it and quickly removed it. "You know how I love to have company, and a friend of yours is always a friend of mine." She wiped her hands down her gown before she grasped Penelope's arm and turned to leave. "I'll get her settled."

Penelope glanced over her shoulder to see Sir Thomas turn and stride back toward his horse with her weapons in hand.

Brithwin intertwined her arm with Penelope's.

"Do you and Thomas go way back?"

Penelope contemplated how to answer the question. "'Tis rather complicated. Our connection goes back many years, aye."

"Sounds mysterious." She grinned, causing her blue eyes to sparkle.

"We are connected by our fathers' encounter. I came in search of Hamon Godfrey and found his son."

"I see. Were your fathers friends, then?"

"Nay, I dinna think one would say that."

Brithwin tipped her head to the side as she turned and looked at Penelope. "I do not mean to pry."

"'Tis fine, milady. I have nothing to hide." The unease of the conversation thickened and settled in Penelope's gut.

"Please, call me Brithwin. And I will call you Penelope." She paused in her steps. "Any friend of Thomas's is a friend of mine."

"But Sir Thomas and I are no' friends, mil—, Brithwin."

"Pshaw. Don't you worry yourself about it, you and I shall be the best of friends while you are here."

Brithwin had to be the most cheery person Penelope had been around in a very long time. But her clan had seen so much death this past year it was not surprising that they had lost their joy.

The lady Brithwin released her arm as they went into the keep through a wooden door. The entry led into the kitchen where a short and stocky woman bent over a table chopping up meat. She looked up as Brithwin and she entered and smiled at her lady. "Good day to you, milady."

"'Tis indeed a good day. The sky is blue, the sun is up, and the birds are singing. But best of all, Thomas has brought us a visitor. Marjory, meet my new friend Penelope."

The woman turned to her and smiled, but her smile faltered as her eyes swept over Penelope's clothing. "Nice to meet you—miss."

"Marjory is a wonderful cook, Penelope. You will not find any better in the north of England." Brithwin boasted of her servant.

The cook's face flushed a brilliant red. She looked down at the meat she'd been chopping. "Why thank you, milady. You are always so kind."

"'Tis the truth and well you know it." Brithwin said the words as she grasped Penelope's arm again and guided her out the kitchen and into the great hall. She glided across the floor with such grace that Penelope felt a twinge of jealousy. For the first time that Penelope could remember she felt awkward in her male clothing. Walking beside this beautiful lady who held herself and walked as if she was royalty, made Penelope wish she could slip away and go off on her own.

Brithwin tugged her to the stairs and the two ascended the flagstone steps. At the top she turned and guided her down a corridor to a door that opened into a solar. "Come in and rest. I will return anon. I must see to the readying of your room."

With that, Brithwin disappeared. Penelope

strolled around the room, looking at the magnificent wall hangings adorning the walls. She fingered each one as she examined the scenes portrayed on the fabric. Passing by the hearth, she ran her hand over the cold stone. The ashes had been swept out and fresh logs lay in the opening waiting for cooler weather.

Today would not be that day. She sat down in a wooden chair with a thick cushion covering the seat and reached for a fan which lay beside it. The day was turning out to be warm and having no breeze flow across the solar only made the air stagnant.

She fanned herself until the heat began to lull her to sleep.

†††

Thomas folded his arms as he looked down at his mistress. He let out a sigh. "Brithwin, have I ever lied to you?"

She took his stance and crossed her arms as she tapped her slippered foot. "Nay, I do not believe you have told me any untruths but today you have run around the whole demesne to throw me off so you do not have to answer me."

Brithwin had been like a daughter to him since her younger years and Thomas had tried to protect her from her wicked father. That is, until her father died and Royce came to Hawkwood. And then it seemed he wanted to protect her from the very man he had desired her to marry.

"I tell you no falsehood, Brithwin. I do not know the lass nor did I know her father." By the rood! He did not want to get into this conversation with her.

"Tell me again, why you have brought her here." She continued to tap her toe, only now it had sped up to a swift beat.

"I do not have time for this conversation. I have many tasks to complete or your husband will come seeking me out." When her brows shot up he groaned inwardly. That argument would not work on her—but there was always another avenue. "Milady, if you would prefer that the lass does not stay here at Hawkwood I am sure I can find other accommodations for her."

She narrowed her eyes to nearly slits and poked her finger at him as she spoke with the authority she had. "You know good and well that I am not asking you to do that. You will not be taking Penelope away from here." She smiled and sweetened her tone. "Besides Thomas, you are not getting any younger. 'Twould be nice if you had someone to look after you just as you looked after me all those years."

Thomas hardened his voice to let her know he would not brook any argument from her. "You'll not be interfering with things while she is at Hawkwood." He knew the lady of Hawkwood better than most anyone here. The only two who may know and understand milady as well as he was Pater and her husband.

Brithwin had mischief up her sleeve. He could see it in the twinkle of her eyes and her insistence on knowing everything that had transpired.

"Me?" Her mouth opened as if in surprise and

her hands flew to her chest.

"Aye, you." He frowned. Her little pretense did not fool him.

Now she frowned. "Thomas Godfrey! I am hurt and disappointed in you that you would think I have some secret motive. I am just so happy to have another lady in the keep and of course because of the connections to you, the man who looked after me and was practically a father to me for all these years, that makes me want to get to know her even more."

Thomas sighed. Perhaps he was too prickly about this lass for some reason. Guilt picked at his conscience. "'Tis sorry I am for being suspicious, Brithwin. It's just…" He stopped there. He'd better not give away one of her traits that let him know she was up to something. Nay, that twinkle in her eye combined with the tapping of her foot was usually a good sign even if he was wrong this time. He'd just keep that to himself.

Her smile returned. "Very well. Then it is settled. Tonight at the evening meal you can fill me in on everything."

Thomas was horrified. "Nay, Milady! I do not think that is a good idea." He heaved another sigh. "What is it you wish to know?"

"But I wish not for you to get in trouble with Royce. I know you do not have time." Her feigned concern did not fool him a bit.

His mistress could be as slippery as a rock in a forest stream. His doubts of her innocent questions resurfaced, but she would be relentless if he did not tell the woman what she wanted to know.

By the time Thomas walked away from Brithwin, though he had avoided the part of Penelope's show of loyalty, he was sure she knew every bit as much as he did about what had transpired and if she had used the same ploy on Penelope, he was certain that she knew more than either him or Penelope individually.

He needed to have a talk with Royce about his wife.

Chapter 4

Penelope had drifted off when the next thing she heard was the heavy wooden door creak open. Forgetting where she was, she jumped to her feet and reached for her sword only to discover it was not there.

An unfamiliar heat rushed up Penelope's neck and into her face as she tried to regain her composure before Sir Thomas stuck his head inside the room. She must have looked like a fool grabbing for her missing sword. His brows knitted in concern, he said nothing, but continued to stare at her. She knew why. Her da had told her many times when she was young that when she flushed with embarrassment her face matched her red rings of hair. But with age and determination she'd learn to overcome the flushing.

"Are you unwell?" Thomas moved into the room.

"Nay, 'tis fine I am. I dozed in the chair. The heat made me drowsy, you see." She bent down and picked up the small hand fan that she now noticed had tumbled to the floor when she rose.

He nodded, but he continued to study her. "The meal is served. Allow me to escort you." He gave a slight bow and swept out his arm toward the door.

"Thank you." She forced a wobbly smile as she continued to try to shake off the uneasiness.

"My pleasure."

"How did you ken where to find me?"

"Milady sent me to fetch you." His words were kind but did it annoy him? He was much too important of a man to be fetching ladies for a meal.

He guided her to the raised dais where the laird and his lady were already seated. Royce stood.

"Milord, allow me to introduce Penelope Beatty. Apparently, our fathers were acquainted. Penelope, allow me to introduce to you, your host, Lord Royce Warwick of Hawkwood."

The laird graciously inclined his head. "'Tis good to meet you."

Penelope realized she was glaring at Sir Thomas rather than greeting her host. Apparently, their fathers were acquainted? She should have known he would not believe her. She turned to the laird and forced a smile as she inclined her head. "I thank you for your hospitality. 'Tis very generous of you."

Brithwin patted a chair beside her. "Come sit. You must be hungry."

Penelope let herself down in the chair next to the lady of the keep. Thomas took a chair down from the laird. The servants brought the trenchers to the table and disappeared back into what she could only imagine was the kitchen, for others exited with more food. She didn't miss the look the laird gave his wife. Brithwin winked and smiled.

"Looks like a fine meal, my love." The laird placed his hand on his wife's and squeezed.

"Aye." Thomas chimed in.

Penelope took a moment to look at the food they placed upon the table. Meat in jelly, fish in a sauce, cooked vegetables, bread, dried fruit, custard, and a most heavenly baked apple that made her mouth water with the aroma of nutmeg and cinnamon.

"Everything looks wonderful, Mi—" Penelope caught the quick glance of Brithwin and corrected herself. "Brithwin. I canno' say I have ever enjoyed such a feast."

The words seemed to please Brithwin and Penelope was glad she'd spoke. Brithwin was young, Penelope determined—many years younger than herself. But the lady seemed much older and wiser than what her sweet face indicated.

Brithwin leaned over and squeezed Penelope's hand just as her husband had done to her and whispered in Penelope's ear. "I do hope you stay. I believe we could be closest of friends. 'Tis my belief we have kindred spirits."

It was the nicest thing anyone had ever said to Penelope. The words filled her with warmth and made her wish she could stay. But staying in England was not something she wanted to do or could do for that matter. She had to get back and help her people.

After the midday meal, Penelope and Brithwin

moved to the solar. Brithwin picked up a small gown and began to stitch on it. For the first time, Penelope looked at her hostess carefully, noticing that she was with child. It was more the glow on the woman's face and the joy in her eyes that caught her attention. "How long before the baby is due?"

"I am thinking six months," she replied, her gaze not leaving the delicate stitches of the baby gown she worked on. "Would you like needle and thread to sew something?"

Penelope held back the chuckle that threatened to bubble up. "I am afraid that is no' one of my skills. Kindred spirits, maybe, but no' in talents."

That answer drew Brithwin's interest and she did raise her head. Penelope stared into the woman's honest eyes. "And being a warrior is one of yours?"

The woman was not looking down on her for being a soldier, Penelope determined, but was honestly curious. Penelope lifted her chin—her pride of her accomplishments welling up within her. "Aye, I am as good a fighter as any man and better than most my size."

Brithwin went back to her sewing. "I see." She continued working on her tiny stitches, as the silence lingered.

The longer the silence continued, the more Penelope worried that perhaps this beautiful woman in her green satin gown with all the delicate embroidery down the front was disappointed in her answer. Why, the woman probably stitched the tapestry that covered the chair she sat on.

Brithwin shook her head in regret. "I always wished I could take care of myself. And quite honestly, I believed I could. But I quickly learned that I am no match for a man. If I would have had your skills, I would never have been captured by Royce's enemy." She put the gown down in her lap and smiled. "But then much would be different and I do not think I would want to change things. God has a way of using things that seem bad and turning them into good. Do not you agree?"

She'd really not given God much thought for a very long time. She was no weak person who needed a god to get her out of trouble. If God cared about her, He never would have let the slaughter happen to her clan. Or at the very least He would have taken her life as well. But she could not tell the mistress of Hawkwood such a thing. She chose to ignore the question. "You were captured by your husband's enemy?"

When their eyes met, Penelope had the feeling she had not fooled Brithwin one jot. But the lovely lady smiled again and answered. "'Tis a long story, but aye, I was a prisoner of a very evil man. I would rather not talk about me, though. I would like to know about you. What really brought you here to Hawkwood?"

"My search for Hamon." Surely Sir Thomas had told the mistress everything.

"But what brought you to your search?"

"Like you, mistress, I was a captive of my enemies. After I escaped I came tae the conclusion I needed help."

That, for some reason had seemed to garner Brithwin's interest. "But you escaped by yourself."

The memories flooded back—the helplessness, the fear, the small child. "Nay, 'twas no' by myself that I escaped. I had help from a child."

Her eyes opened wide then Brithwin's brow wrinkled. "A child you say?"

Penelope smiled, now in the safety of the English keep. "Aye. A small boy had lost his way and I convinced him if he would free me that I would help him find his home. I had nearly given up hope when the child completed his task and I was freed."

"Did you help him find his way back to his mother?" Brithwin caressed the satin material over her abdomen, and the worried look in her eyes let Penelope know that much weight rested on her answer.

"Aye, I always keep my promises. 'Tis the honorable thing tae do."

"Were you not concerned that you would be found?"

"Very much so. But I had given my word. I would no' go back on it."

At that moment Penelope knew she'd been weighed, judged and found worthy. It shouldn't have mattered but it made her happy that Brithwin approved of her.

"What are your plans now, Penelope? Do you wish to go back to your home?"

Visions of the slaughter of her clan rolled through her memory. The agonizing screams, the metallic smell of blood, the look of death, all came flooding back for her to relive and sent chills up her spine.

"I have no home or people tae go back tae." For one of them had betrayed her and she didn't know who. She couldn't go back and risk being turned over to the enemy again. At least until she formed some sort of a plan.

"So, you will stay here with Thomas?"

Penelope nearly choked, coughing for a moment before she could catch her breath. "Nay. I am no' with Thomas. But I wish tae stay here, Milady, with your permission, until 'tis safe for me tae return tae Scotland. I dinna ken how long that will be."

"You are welcome to stay as long as you would like." Brithwin gave her a knowing smile. "Me thinks not only I would like that but a certain knight would too."

Penelope frowned as she tried to think of a knight whom she'd had contact with who showed her any interest. No one came to mind. She shook her head. "I ken no' of whom you speak, milady."

Brithwin threw her head back and laughed as if someone had told her the funniest story. "Can you not see admiration in my master-at-arms' eyes?"

"Sir Thomas?" Penelope choked out the name in disbelief.

"Of course." Brithwin answered as she went back to her delicate stitching.

"Oh my. You have misread your master-at-arms' intentions. The man can barely tolerate me. Why, if it had no' been for the promise of his father's, he would have sent me on my way faster than an arrow releases from a bow."

Brithwin looked up from beneath her perfectly shaped eyebrows. "You do not know Thomas as I know Thomas."

"'Tis true. I dinna. But if you saw the way the man looks at me. You would think otherwise." Truly, the man could barely stand to look at her. It was obvious he loathed her being a warrior. She shrugged, trying not to let the thought bother her, all the while chastising herself for even caring.

The day dragged on and Brithwin excused herself to oversee the evening meal. Penelope wandered around the keep, putting to memory where the different rooms were and where she found the best escape route.

She slowed as she passed a window that overlooked the practice field. Giving in to temptation, she stopped and rested her hands on the wooden sill. A battle drill ensued across the way, reminding her that she neither had her dirk or her sword. She sighed, wishing she could join the men in their mock melee. The clanging of swords, the shouts of orders, and moments of laughter, only made her miss her home and her clansmen more.

Her eyes were drawn to Hawkwood's master-at-arms. Though some of the men were younger than his thirty-five-ish years, it was obvious why the laird kept Thomas as his master-of-arms. Not wanting to get caught watching the men, Penelope contemplated searching out Brithwin to see if she could help her with something. The men stopped their sword play and seemed to be having either a challenge or a disagreement, or perhaps both.

A large circle formed and a short discussion ensued as five men stepped into the circle. Penelope waited for the second group of five to enter the circle, sure that she knew the five were about to battle one on one with five other men.

First the laird stepped into the ring followed by Sir Thomas. Penelope waited for the other three men, but none joined them. She frowned thinking she had misunderstood what was about to take place and waited to find out. She'd not waited long, for a battle cry went out and the five knights moved in on the laird and the master-at-arms.

Penelope clenched her lower lip between her front teeth as the men went into hand-to-hand combat. It mattered not who won the silly game but her heart pulled for the two outnumbered men. Expecting to see them dispatched quickly, she was pleasantly surprised that they seemed to be holding their own. As time went on, Penelope expected Royce and Thomas to tire and call it perhaps a draw. However, once again the two men outdid themselves and she witnessed several of the five making foolish mistakes and having to pull themselves up from the ground.

She should leave to find Brithwin, but she couldn't pull herself away as the game wound down. A smile tugged at the corner of her lips when another and then another fell. As the last man staggered away before collapsing to his knees, she realized that they had won today's tussle. And by the laughing, shoving, and slaps on the back, she'd wager that this challenge was a regular event.

Chapter 5

A group of highland warriors with the late afternoon sun at their backs, faced Thomas and Royce. They had emerged from the western woods as Thomas and Royce trudged up to the outer gate. Both men stopped and faced the Scotsmen who'd laid down their various weapons.

Thomas stood next to Royce, with arms folded across his chest. One man moved to the front of the group and approached Thomas and Royce.

Royce didn't wait for them to speak. "What would you be doing on Hawkwood land?"

He and Royce had just returned from the village and checking up on a small feud between neighbors when they saw the Scotsmen approach. They'd come with a small arsenal but none now stood with a weapon in his possession. At least that is what these men were leading them to believe. Thomas scrutinized each man, looking for hidden knives before searching behind them at the tree line to see if any men hid away in hopes of getting the upper hand. It wouldn't be the first time someone had tried such a ploy.

The blond-headed leader in tattered clothes stopped just outside of a hand's reach. "We come in peace. We search for someone."

Royce cocked his head. "Peace you say? With that kind of arsenal? You must be looking for a small army."

Thomas gave a quick glance behind him to see that the wall armaments stood at the ready.

"I am Alban." The man who'd stepped to the front of the men spoke. "We are no' here tae fight ye or any army. We look for only one."

Thomas's brows shot up. "You have," Thomas scanned the group a second time to make sure his count had been correct. "Eight men all highly armed and you search for only one man?"

It was hard to believe the man spoke the truth to them coming on to English soil looking like they were ready for war.

The man looked down at his feet and shuffled them a bit. "Nay, 'twould be a lass whom we search for."

Thomas leaned his head forward and turned his ear toward the man, thinking he'd heard him wrong. "Did you say a lass?"

The man nodded, not lifting his eyes to Thomas. Royce let out a guffaw and quickly turned it into a coughing spell. Though he fooled no one. Thomas couldn't help but grin. "So would this lass be a giant?"

Royce chuckled again. Alban narrowed his eyes,

pinching three small wrinkles between them. "She is no' just any lass. She is an opponent who can disappear afor yer eyes. She can sneak up silently while ye sleep and slice yer throat."

Thomas shook his head while fighting to keep the humor out of his voice. "Sounds more like fairy magic to me."

"Nay." One of the men behind Alban spoke up. "The lass can disappear like a fairy but she is much more cunning. And as strong as the Bible's Samson. 'Tis said if ye could cut the lass's red curly locks she would be as weak as a bairn."

Thomas swung his gaze to Royce. The humor fled his being. He read the same thoughts in Royce's eyes. Penelope.

Alban apparently saw the look between the two. "Do ye ken the lass of which we speak?"

Thomas shrugged, trying not to show any concern. "I know no fairy lass. Do you, Royce?"

"Nay." Royce replied as he bent over and picked a blade of grass from the ground and stuck it in his mouth. "Does this lass have a name?"

Alban nodded his head with great enthusiasm. "Penelope Beatty."

Thomas gave a grunt as thoughts whirled through his mind. The lass had better not pop her head up on the rampart to see what was going on out here. He did not wish to dispatch these men and it was difficult to say if any others hid further back in the woods. "Does not sound like a fairy name to me." He responded.

"We told ye 'tis no fairy but she surely has

magical powers tae do the things of a man." Alban's irritation was evident with his rising pitch.

Royce pulled the piece of grass from his mouth. "We know no fairies and no magical lassies. But should we see her we will be sure to tell her you seek her."

Alban scratched his scruffy blond beard. "I be thinking that might no' be a guid idea. It would be best if ye came and told us."

"If we see a magical fairy lass with red hair I will send one of my men to alert you." Royce gave a sharp snap of his head as if to confirm his words.

Alban nodded as if satisfied. The man who'd spoken earlier mumbled something about 'tis no' fairy lass, as he turned to walk away.

Thomas and Royce didn't move as they watched the men depart, disappearing into the copse of trees. When the Scots could be seen no more, the two turned and headed through the portcullis that had been raised for them.

Royce turned his head toward Thomas and examined him as they walked into the outer bailey.

"What?" Thomas asked defensively.

"Nothing." Royce grinned.

"Do not tell me 'tis nothing. I see something in your eyes."

Royce laughed. "Me wife tells me that you finally have found a woman worthy of you. I just wonder what you now think of this woman who has men trembling in their boots."

Thomas let out a growl. "I have been meaning to talk to you about that wife of yours."

Royce interrupted. "Oh no, my friend, you are the one who practically raised her. I am the recipient of your fine work."

"The woman needs to learn her place. There is little she will not do to get her way."

"Oh aye. Brithwin always finds a way to get what she wants. She is a master at that. And a good husband will delight in giving it to her. But do not forget, the Lord can change hearts of women or men that seem bent on having their own way. Yet it seems you have avoided my question. What do you think of this Penelope now?"

Thomas grunted. "Me thinks she too, needs to learn her place."

Royce's good-natured chuckle ended abruptly, causing Thomas to see why. Less than a horse's length stood Penelope with Brithwin beside her.

"Come wife, I am in need of your company." Royce put his arm around Brithwin's shoulders but before he led her away, he turned to him. "Thomas, remember my words. 'Tis not only women."

Thomas was thankful for his lord's interference. At least part of his interference. He did not want to deal with Brithwin at the moment. He had other things on his mind. Like the slender red head standing before him with arms crossed.

"My enemy still seeks me. He will no' stop until…"

Thomas grasped her elbow and the two began to walk. "Until what?"

"'Tis nothing. They are a determined bunch. I should no' stay here. They must suspect this is where I have come."

"Nay, they only inquired. We told them we had not seen a fairy warrior." He smiled trying to ease her worries.

"'Twas not my intention tae bring harm or danger tae your people."

"You have brought no such thing upon Hawkwood. They do not suspect you are here. And 'twas only a handful of men. They can do no harm to us. You have seen our fortresses and our men. They are like ants to us."

"This is what you believe but I ken these men. They may not attack your fortress, but they will lie in wait for one or two of you tae leave and then they will move."

"Ah, lass, you worry too much. As I said they have gone elsewhere to look for you. They will not be back."

"I hope you are right." She reached down and felt the empty case she'd kept her dirk in before sliding her hand over to a small pouch hanging off her belt.

"You miss your weapons?"

"Aye. I feel naked without them."

"Why? You are surrounded by seasoned knights. Every one of them would lay down their life for you, including myself." Thomas studied the half warrior, half woman who walked beside him. How could someone so beautiful want to be a soldier?

"I wish no man tae lay his life down for me. I protect myself. I need no one." She hesitated and gave a quick glance his way before ducking her head. "Or at least I try. I ken I came here for your protection."

She seemed to put up a front of a mighty fighter. And perhaps she handled a weapon better than most women. But this lass was no warrior. She needed a real man to care for her. Thomas found himself wanting to pull her into his arms and ease the lines of worry furrowed on her brow. "And my protection you will have. No one will touch you here. I will see to that."

Chapter 6

Penelope found herself warring within. She had been at Hawkwood a little over a fortnight and no one knew the truth about why these people would not give up. No matter what Thomas said, she knew how much the ones who sought her wanted the cross that rest in the hat's crown that hung on the pole of her bed. It would be worth a king's ransom to any man who possessed it. Aye, that was the truth of it. A man, not a woman.

She would not put these kind people into harm's way for her safety. If her enemy returned, she would leave—with or without Thomas's blessing. He was a kind man, but like so many he could not accept her as who she was. She peeked out of the corner of her eye at him. Pity. She did not want his pity. Why did men think all women were helpless creatures who couldn't care for themselves?

The thought annoyed her. She would have to show Thomas that she was quite capable of looking after herself. She'd just have to figure out how. The next time she saw Brithwin, she'd enquire of her. The woman had a sound head on her shoulders and between the two of them they would come up with something.

They approached the mews and Penelope slowed. A man stepped out of the building with a bird balanced on his gauntlet. Peeking behind him and inside the mews, she could see tall perches situated into the sandy ground. Her attention was drawn back to the falconer as he removed the hood from the blue-gray Peregrine falcon, showing its beautiful dark head.

The majestic bird fluffed out its wings and puffed up its white and black barred chest. Penelope let out a sigh as she admired the exquisite bird. The falconer spoke quietly to the creature and as if it understood, it calmed before her eyes.

"His name is Talon. He is Milady's." Thomas, standing beside her, broke the silence.

"He is so beautiful. I have never owned a bird."

"Aye, he is one of milady's favorites."

After a few moments the falconer raised his hand and gave a flick of his wrist. The bird lifted into the air. The falconer then threw a piece of meat, sending it sailing through the air and falling into high grass. Penelope watched with excitement as Talon swooped down and landed in the tall brush, almost concealing his identity. To her delight, when Talon flew back to his trainer he had clutched in his talons the chunk of meat. The falconer took the meat and handed it to the bird.

"Perhaps someday you would like to go out

hawking?" Thomas asked.

"I have never been."

He nodded.

He placed his hand behind the small of her back and guided her toward the mews. "Would you like to see the other birds?"

The heat of his hand on her back sent shivers up her spine. It had been at least ten years since a man had touched her so intimately. They were more likely to slap her on the back for a good shot. The unfamiliar feeling caused her stomach to swirl. What was happening to her? She long ago had made the decision she'd never marry. Now here she was feeling like a young girl looking for a husband. "I should see if Brithwin needs my help."

She needed to get away—to breathe.

"Brithwin is with her husband." He winked at her. "'Tis sure I am that she will not need your help."

Heat once again filled her face. Heavens! There she went again. She had long ago learned to control her embarrassment.

He lifted his hand and brushed the back of his finger against her cheek. "Ah, so smooth. Your beauty belies the warrior garb you wear."

His kind words drew her in and she gazed into his near black eyes. She should get angry... but his gentle touch seemed to soothe the wound of his comment. What she wanted was to close her eyes, and enjoy the closeness. But though she did not pull away, she wouldn't give in to that desire.

"Your blush is becoming on you." His whisper

caused the wisps of hair on the side of her face to tickle her cheek.

She reached up and pushed the hair away coming to herself. "I never blush."

His hand dropped as she turned her head away. And suddenly she regretted her actions.

"Nay. I do not imagine you do." The softness had left his voice and the amusement was back. It was as if he returned to the Thomas she'd met a fortnight ago. "Let me at least show you Lioness. 'Tis Milady's other falcon."

Thomas led her between the perches to a smaller Peregrine falcon, resting with its eyes closed.

"This is Lioness. Brithwin thought she might lose this bird at one time, it was so sick. But they nursed her back to health and as you can see, she is quite fit."

Penelope lifted her hand to stroke the bird's feathers and stopped. "May I?"

"Aye, she will not bite."

She ran her hand down the sleek cool feathers and the bird leaned into her touch. "She likes it." She said in surprise.

"Brithwin spends much time with her falcons. They are familiar with her touch. You must have the same gift."

"I think I would be tempted tae do the same if I owned such magnificent creatures. Spend much time with them, that is."

"Me thinks that is much how The Master thinks. He loves spending time with His Bride when she is still and quiet."

She knew he tested her, to see if she knew of which he spoke. She chose to let him wonder. "I needs to be on my way."

"Then I will leave you to seek out milady." He tilted his head and cocked an eyebrow as a smile played on the corner of his lips.

She knew he insinuated that Brithwin would still be with her husband. She refused to play into his humor. "I do have things I would like tae do."

He extended his arm toward the door. She quietly slipped out, making sure not to disturb the other falcons alit on their perches. She glanced over her shoulder as she exited to see Thomas stroking Lioness. Though she departed, her thoughts would not leave the tall man she'd left in the mews.

Penelope went to the room she had been given while at Hawkwood. She needed to think. These feelings swirling around in her stomach were not welcome. She'd made her decision ten years ago that she would be nothing more than a warrior. She would not marry. She would not have children. She would submit to no man. It was and would always be she who chose her destiny.

Pacing around the room only to stop and glance out the window helped her to pass the time. Brithwin would surely be returning to the keep shortly to oversee the evening meal. The sun dipped low in the sky, which meant she should already have returned. She flopped into one of the two chairs sitting before the fireplace. Weariness of having nothing to do seized her. To be able to practice with her sword, bow, and dirk would ease the feeling of wanting to jump out of her skin.

Waiting. That was all she could do. She'd never been very good about that. It had gotten her into trouble a few times in her life. And if she was honest with herself, she supposed that was part of the reason she decided not to marry. It kept her from having to wait for the right man to come along—or worry that he never would.

A soft rap on the door drew her out of her thoughts.

"'Tis Brithwin."

"Come in." Penelope stood but Brithwin was in the door and gliding across the room before she could take more than a step.

"Thomas said you look for me." Brithwin made her way to the chair sitting opposite. She swooped her arm under her gown and sank down onto the chair with elegance.

Heat rose in Penelope cheeks and she willed it away. "I wished tae help you in some way— perhaps in the kitchen."

Brithwin batted her hand toward her. "I have already seen to the evening meal. So we have time for a visit. Have I told you how much I enjoy you staying here?"

"Thank you, Milady." Penelope looked down at her hands folded in her lap.

"Ah, ah, ah. I am Brithwin." She shook her finger back and forth at her.

The kindness in Brithwin's words warmed her heart. "Thank you, Brithwin."

"I do mean it. And I hope you feel the same way

about your visit here."

"Oh, I do. 'Tis immensely I enjoy your company. You have been so vera kind and welcoming tae me."

Brithwin cocked her head. "And Thomas."

It wasn't a question. At least she didn't think it was. But she should clarify. "'Twas guid of Thomas tae…" What exactly had Thomas done for her? Nothing really. She'd found her way here. "Offer Hawkwood as a place of refuge." There! She'd thought of something.

"I have noticed over the past sennights that our Thomas is quite taken with you."

"Me? Oh nay, Mila—Brithwin, you are sorely mistaken. The man can scarcely look at me most of the time."

Brithwin let out a loud and unladylike laugh just as another knock sounded behind them.

"Aye?" Brithwin answered the knock taking it out of Penelope's hands.

"'Tis Thomas."

Penelope started to rise.

"Come in Thomas." Brithwin waved her back down onto her seat. "What brings you to Penelope's room?"

Penelope cringed at the playfulness in Brithwin's voice.

Thomas straightened. He looked as if he would chastise the lady of the manor, but instead let out a sigh. "I just spoke with your husband and he informed me that I would find you here with Penelope."

"Penelope?" Brithwin challenged the familiarity of which he spoke as she sat forward in her seat, the mischief not leaving her voice.

He glared at the mistress. "She is a warrior, milady." He ground out the words between clenched teeth.

Brithwin laughed, her voice as sweet to the ears as tinkling glass. "Mmm. That she is. But she is also a lady."

Penelope could only imagine how uncomfortable Thomas had to be because she wanted to crawl under the chair.

Thomas continued to glare at his mistress as he moved into the room and toward them. "I came to deliver Lady Penelope her weapons."

Her weapons? Penelope sprang up from her chair and met him halfway. "Thank you!" She may have sounded a bit over zealous—but her weapons!

"My, my Thomas. You do know the way to a lady's heart, don't you?" Brithwin teased.

Penelope glanced up and thought she actually saw a blush seeping into Thomas's cheeks from beneath his short beard.

"She mentioned missing her things. I thought it would help her feel…comfortable. Your husband gave me permission to return them to her."

"'Twas vera kind of you tae ask him." Penelope interjected before Brithwin could have more sporting fun with Thomas. She found herself feeling sorry for the man.

"Aye, Thomas, 'twas very kind." Brithwin mimicked.

"If you ladies will excuse me. I have things to oversee." Thomas gave a slight bow and left the room before either of them could say another word.

Brithwin fell back into her chair, her laughter filling the room.

"Brithwin!"

Penelope couldn't help but chuckle herself.

"What?" she said innocently.

"The poor man. You caused him so much grief."

Brithwin had a hard time getting a hold of her laughter. "He deserves it! The man caused me much the same when he all but forced me to marry Royce."

"Forced you? That is barbaric."

Brithwin shrugged. "Well, maybe not truly forced. But he used tactics that put me under pressure. Tactics he knew would convince me. He used the safety of my people against me. Warning me that I needed someone like Royce to protect them. He even had the gall to send a letter to the king, informing him that it would be a welcome marriage."

"But you and Royce seem so happy—so in love." Penelope couldn't believe that these two hadn't married out of love.

"Aye, we are—now. But it did not start out that way. I was not so willing to relinquish my position in the keep. And Royce, well he did not take kindly to my obstinacy. But eventually he came around." She giggled.

"I see. So, if it were no' for Thomas, you and Royce would no' be together."

"Oh, I would not say that. The Lord has a way of bringing people together when He wants to. And I do believe Royce and I were meant for each other. So you see, it is my right to torment Thomas over the woman he will marry."

Penelope almost swallowed her tongue. "Married tae me? Surely you jest. Have you so quickly forgotten what I just told you, that Thomas does no' much care for the sight of me?"

Brithwin shook her head in argument. "Penelope, I do hope I will not offend you, but you have been living like a man too long if you cannot see that Thomas is indeed taken with you. Now, I will give you that he does not know what to do about it. I would imagine because he has never been interested in a woman with your skills. Thus, he brought you your weapons."

It was strange how something she'd been thinking about only hours earlier would get brought up in a conversation. Penelope hated to dampen her new friend's enthusiasm, but she needed to set her straight.

"And I dinna wish tae offend you, Lady Brithwin, but I choose me own destiny. Not God. And I made the decision when I was a young lass that I would be a warrior—not a wife."

Chapter 7

Thomas leaned his shoulder against a tree outside of the keep, feeling like he'd just battled ten men and couldn't catch his breath. If he had his way Royce would have a good sit down talk with his wife. He might even encourage him to put her over his knee. He chuckled. No, Royce would never hurt Brithwin. That was part of the reason he'd chosen him for her. She'd had enough pain growing up under an abusive father.

He sure would have liked to have given her a piece of his mind after her impudence. Suggesting in front of Penelope none-the-less that he returned the lass's weapons as some sort of romantic gesture. He just might have to get Brithwin by herself and give her the stern talking to that she needed.

He shook his head in hopelessness. But if the woman got something in her mind, heaven forbid, it was downright impossible to sway her. He'd have to avoid her—at least when she was around Penelope. The last thing he needed was to give her opportunities to play the matchmaker. As much as milady thought he needed a helpmate, he knew he was too old and set in his ways to think about marriage. He was too old to train a wife. And Lord have mercy on him should he choose a woman who fought like a man. No, staying single and caring for Hawkwood was his life's ambition.

He snorted as he pushed away from the tree. Out of all the women for Brithwin to fixate on it was a woman who dressed as a man and fought with men. What was his mistress thinking when she said he needed someone to take care of him? Did she think he needed a woman to protect him? He shook his head. If he wanted a woman, which he didn't, it certainly wouldn't be a hardened warrior. Unless, as Royce had mentioned, the Lord could change her ways.

Thomas trudged off to find Royce and plead with him in hopes he would at least consider talking to that wife of his. He found him with his friend Jarren Bourne speaking to a merchant who'd brought in a wagon full of fine linens, spices, and a sword that Jarren seemed to be coveting.

Jarren glanced up from the sword as he caressed the handle with his thumb. "'Tis a fine arming sword."

Thomas eyed the piece in the knight's hands, realizing why the weapon had found favor with Jarren. Every part of the hilt, the guard, grip, and pommel had extra care and embellishment on it. He let out a low whistle. The guard curved upward with delicate leaf scrolling along the sides which both had carved on them roaring lion heads. The grip had a carved rope crisscross to form three X's, and the pommel had the same leaf scrolling which encircled a raised cross. "Fine indeed."

Letting the sword rest across all eight fingers, Jarren extended his arms, offering the blade to Thomas.

"'Twould be a beautiful wedding gift for such a bonnie lass." Jarren let out a chortle at his own joke.

Any desire to pick up and examine the sword fled with Jarren's words. Royce had stopped speaking mid- sentence and focused on him. Thomas burned inside. Had Brithwin gone around to everyone spilling her foolishness?

Thomas raised a single brow refusing to bite. "Well now, Jarren, if you are looking for a warrior wife I know one I can introduce you to."

Jarren grinned. "She would not be such a bad catch. Comely and she would always have my back in battle."

A brilliant idea developed and Thomas returned Jarren's smile. "'Today is your lucky day, my friend." Thomas slapped him on the back. "It seems it has become milady's ambition in life to find a mate for Penelope. I will head her way now to give her the good news."

Jarren's smile faded as Thomas spun on his heel.

"Nay, Thomas, I referred to you."

Thomas continued to walk, ignoring Jarren's protests.

"Royce," Thomas heard Jarren from over his

shoulder. "Tell him I am not interested in having a warrior as a wife."

The roar of Royce's laughter reminded Thomas of the two lion heads on the hilt guard. He smiled. Problem solved. He'd just inform Brithwin that Penelope had an admirer.

He didn't find Brithwin alone for near on a sennight. Every time he saw her, Penelope was at her side and he headed in the opposite direction. Whenever Royce was around and saw him scurrying away like a critter running from a predator, he'd let out a chuckle and all Thomas could do was glare at him.

But this fine day Milady worked in her garden and the woman was nowhere to be seen.

"Good day, Brithwin. 'Tis a fine day to work with your flowers." He stopped beside her and clasped his hands behind his back.

She gave a quick glance up and went back to pulling weeds. "Aye. Fine indeed. What can I help you with today, Thomas?"

"I am in need of nothing. I saw you out here and—"

"And you saw I was alone so you thought to speak.to me? Think not that I am unaware of you avoiding me or should I say Penelope?"

Thomas had the urge to shuffle his feet like a child getting a good scolding but refused to let his mistress lower him to such things. He'd not have had to avoid her if she'd have minded her own business.

"I see you are a wee bit upset with me. I bring

you good news and hopefully it will cheer you." And set your cupid skills on someone else, he thought to himself.

"Aye?" She paused in her work and looked at him intently.

"I spoke with Jarren the other day." He took a deep breath to plunge on.

"Aye. I spoke to Jarren, myself. Yesterday. It seems there was some sort of a misunderstanding between you two."

†††

Today was the first day that Penelope had practiced with her bow since she'd arrived. Releasing the string to hear it slice through the air and watching it shoot the arrow directly into her target was exhilarating. It had taken her some time to find a place where she could practice and would not be gawked at by a passerby.

She had just finished shooting when the crack of a branch sent her nocking another arrow as she swung around.

"Do no' shoot." The man yelled out and stopped.

She recognized the man as one of the knights from Hawkwood. Another broke through the trees the first had come through.

She didn't lower her weapon. "Did you come tae spy on me?"

The first man shrugged. "I came to see if the rumors were true about you. I am Elfed and my friend here is Adam."

The man hovering near the treeline gave her a

nod.

"What did you hear?" She asked.

"That you are a fairy lass and you can disappear." Elfed smiled.

"Weel, as you can see, I have no' disappeared." She released the tension on the string and lowered the bow.

"Tis said you can shoot as well or better than a man and throw a dirk the same." Elfed laughed.

Penelope glanced to Adam who still hadn't moved, then back to Elfed. "Aye, 'tis true."

"Ha!" No female can shoot or throw as well as a man." Elfed goaded.

"I am not so sure, Elfed. You saw her shoot." Adam finally spoke.

"Come now, Adam." Elfed spun around and faced his friend. "You are not afeared of a woman are you?"

"Nay. I only say that I saw her shoot."

"You may not think you can best her in a shot but I ken I can." Elfed boasted.

"That did sound like a challenge, Milady." Adam moved forward. "Perhaps you and he should have a contest."

Elfed's grin irritated her. Though she was not one to have contests to prove her skill, she found it hard to turn this one down.

She shrugged. "If you insist. But dinna get angry with me when you find yourself losing tae a woman."

"I think we should have a wager on this."

Elfed went back in the woods and came out with

a bow. It appeared the man may have planned this all out. She sighed.

"I do not ken if I would do that, Elfed." Adam cautioned.

"Aye, we dinna need tae—"

"Are you afeared you will lose, lass?" Elfed again goaded.

"Nay. As you wish. But I dinna have money." Penelope did not like to wager on anything—even if it was a sure thing—for someone ended up unhappy or angry.

"Your dirk and bow if you lose. One arrow and whoever gets it the closest to the target center wins." Elfed pointed to the weapon in her hand.

"And what will you give?" Adam inquired.

"My sword."

"Are you sure you want to do that? Royce will no' be pleased if you have no sword." Adam warned.

"Do you think I will lose? I do no' plan to."

"'Tis always best to err on the side of caution." Adam advised.

"Be off with you." Elfed dismissed his friend's concerns.

Adam shook his head but didn't appear to be going anywhere.

"'Tis a fair trade." Penelope looked at Elfed. "You may pick our targets."

"Do you see the knot on yonder tree?" He pointed to a tree beyond which she'd been shooting.

She nodded.

"Do you wish to go first, milady?" He smirked.

"Nay. You may go first."

He let out a chortle. "Do you think a few more moments will help you?" He nocked his arrow, and took his stance. He held the bow still as he took aim and then released the string. The arrow sailed through the air and hit its target. "Ha! Do you wish to concede now and save yourself the humiliation?"

"I shall take my chances." Penelope nocked her arrow, quickly took aim and let the arrow go. Her arrow hit the knot as well.

"Woo! Looks to be a tie to me." A hint of excitement sounded in Adam's voice.

"Nay. We will see who got closer to the center of the knot. For I aimed for the center." Elfed started toward the tree.

Penelope followed. "I did as well."

As they neared the tree, Adam ran ahead. "Looks to me as the lass won. Her arrow is square in the middle."

"Let me see." Elfed pushed him out of the way and looked. "'Twas luck!"

"The same could be said about you hitting the knot." Penelope replied a bit irritated.

"Let us shoot one more time. This time further away." Elfed pulled his arrow from the tree.

Penelope sighed. It would not end well for Elfed. "As you wish."

Adam wedged a leaf in the bark of a tree that was about one and a half times further than the first tree. Elfed and Penelope went back to the spots they first shot from. This time Elfed did not ask her if she wished to go first. He nocked his arrow and took aim. When he released it, the arrow sailed through the air and again met its target.

He sneered at her. "Let us now see who the better archer is."

Penelope nocked her arrow and took her aim and let the arrow release. It too, hit its mark. Adam dashed off ahead and Elfed darted behind him. When she reached the tree, there was silence. She looked to the leaf. Her arrow once again hit the center of its target. Elfed's arrow caught the edge.

"'Twas luck again I tell you!" Elfed yelled. "I wish to repeat this. A breeze caught my arrow. Did you not feel the wind when I shot?" He asked Adam.

"'Tis no' necessary." Penelope interjected. "I dinna want you sword. 'Tis of no use tae me. All I ask is you dinna spread this all over Hawkwood"

Adam chuckled. "You do no' have to worry with that, lass. I do no' think Elfed will be telling anyone."

Elfed glared at Adam. "And you do no' need to be telling tales yourself."

Adam wiggled his brows. "Oh, I will be telling no tales, only the truth."

Penelope giggled. "I must get back and see if Brithwin needs my help."

With that, she headed back the path she took— to Hawkwood.

Chapter 8

Penelope found Brithwin in the solar. "Guid day tae you." She said cheerfully.

"And good day to you, Penelope. I hoped you would seek me out." Brithwin sat sewing on a new project. "Come in and join me."

Penelope sat in the chair across from her friend. "Did you finish the baby's gown?"

"I did. Would you like to see it?" She rose from her chair, not waiting for Penelope's reply.

"I imagine 'tis lovely. You do such beautiful work." Penelope lifted her voice as Brithwin stepped into another room.

"I am pleased you think so." She reentered the room with a gown fit for royalty.

Penelope couldn't hold back the gasp. "'Tis so beautiful. Such delicate stitches." She fingered the needlework. "'Tis perfect. Your child will be the envy of young and old."

A slight blush colored Brithwin's cheeks. "Thank you. I always find so many flaws in my work."

Penelope smiled. "Oh, milady—Brithwin, 'tis truly gorgeous. Anyone would be proud tae wear something you have sewn."

A gleam came into the mistress's eyes. "I am so pleased to hear you say that. I've been working on something for you."

Holding her smile in place was a struggle. "For me?" She could only hope she sounded pleased.

Brithwin disappeared back into the other room with the gown and returned without it.

"Aye. I know you only came with the clothes on your back and you have had to have them washed at night to wear clean clothes the next day. I believe you and I are near the same size." She grinned. "Other than you are a wee bit taller. So I took the liberty of finding one of my dresses and adding some length to the bottom." She sashayed over to where she'd been working on the new project and held up the skirt of the dress.

The azure linen fabric with the white floral embroidery nearly took her breath away.

"I used linen. I thought since you weren't used to wearing a gown, silk might not be comfortable for you." Brithwin hurried on. "I know you do not wear dresses but I thought it would be nice since you will have no need to use your weapons while you are here."

The words would not come out. Even if they would have, she had no words in her mind to say. Her thoughts whirled and she willed it to stop so she could make sense of things. A dress? Her? Why she'd not worn one of those contraptions since she'd made her mind up to defend her people.

Brithwin seemed to have trouble with the lingering silence. "And I have no breeches or tunic and sure I am that Royce's would be much too large. And it was really quite simple for me to put this scalloped fabric on the bottom of my gown to add length."

The woman was rambling. She really needed to put her mind to ease. "'Tis fine, Brithwin. You need not explain yourself."

Brithwin let out a whoosh of air from her lungs. "Thank goodness because I was running out of reasons."

Penelope had to admire her honesty. Could she be so honest? Brithwin deserved nothing less. Hesitantly, she walked over to the gown still in Brithwin's hands and fingered the fabric. She'd done a lovely job adding the five or so inches to the bottom of the gown. One would not know that it had not been made that way. She'd even added the beautiful embroidery to the new scalloped hem.

"I dinna wish tae hurt your feelings." She stopped, thinking perhaps there was a better way to proceed. "You have done a lovely job. I couldno' tell this piece was added if you'd no' told me. Truly, Brithwin, 'tis vera nice indeed. However, I dinna wear a gown."

Brithwin gave her a big smile. "Weel, I must admit I did notice that."

Penelope laughed. "Aye, I imagine you did."

Brithwin sank into her chair, and nodded to her

to sit.

"A gown is really not so cumbersome, Penelope. And since you have no other clothes…"

Oh, she did not want to have this conversation. "I would no' be comfortable in a dress. I have no' worn one for ten or more years."

Brithwin's eyes widened before she gained her composure. "Then what a perfect time! Your time is your own while you are here."

The woman was persistent, Penelope would give her that. "I appreciate your kindness, but—"

"'Twould please Thomas, of that I am sure."

"So we are back tae that. I tell you the truth, Thomas has no warm feelings toward me. He has helped me only because his father owed my Da a favor."

Brithwin's smile was telling. "And may I remind you that you do not know Thomas as I do. He is good at putting on a false front. But you have captivated the man."

"As I told you, I chose tae be a defender of the people over a wife. I need no' impress your Thomas. There is no need tae."

Leaning forward, Brithwin rested her hands in her lap. "Why do you need to choose one or the other?"

Penelope couldn't hold in the sardonic laugh. "No man wishes to marry a woman who fights as well as he."

"I doubt you have to concern yourself with that. Thomas is one of our best knights. I have no doubt you are a fine warrior, Penelope, but few match my husband and Thomas on the sparring field."

To her chagrin, her friend spoke the truth. Hadn't she watched the two men defeat five during practice? She smiled to cover her embarrassment. "'Tis true. They are skilled knights."

"Now with that out of the way, you need not choose between warrior and marriage."

"Marriage is no' the path I have chosen, milady."

"But it *can* be. Can you honestly tell me that Thomas holds no interest for you?"

"He is a handsome man tae be sure. But I dinna let my mind wander down those roads. 'Tis of no use. I made my choice."

"Aye, but that was before you knew there was a choice." She scooted to the edge of her chair and Penelope had the feeling she was about to pounce. "What I am saying is you do have a choice now. I see no reason you cannot have both. I have known Thomas since I was a young girl when he was newly knighted. You have caught the man's eye, Penelope, of that I am sure."

Penelope let her mind go down those paths she'd avoided her whole adult life. A husband. It was a hard thing to fathom, she'd lived in denial of that so long. If Sir Thomas was interested in her as a woman, how did she feel about that? Why, she'd not know how to conduct herself in the fashion befitting a woman.

"Please." Brithwin pleaded. "At least try the dress on."

With a sigh from Penelope, Brithwin took it as

an aye. And before she could protest, the lady of the manor had ushered her into her room, closed the door and helped her don the azure gown.

Brithwin stood back and clasped her hands in front of her. "It fits wonderfully! I knew it would. And you look beautiful." She twirled her finger around. "Let me see the back."

Penelope obliged her and spun around slowly. She had to admit the contraption with all its layers was not nearly as uncomfortable as she had imagined it would be.

"Perfect!" Brithwin clapped her hands, grinning ear to ear. "Now sit down and let me do something with your hair."

Before she could protest, Brithwin had pushed her down onto a small chair and snatched a comb off a side table. Penelope plaited her hair into a single long braid much of the time to keep her curls under control. But she could tell under Brithwin's administrations, the woman was choosing something much different.

Brithwin rushed over to the wall and pulled a reflecting glass from it. Her slippered feet padded a soft tapping on the way back. She held the reflecting glass before Penelope. "You look so beautiful." Her voice softened with the words.

Penelope looked at herself. Brithwin had braided her hair and wound it around her head to form a crown.

"Stand up." Brithwin stepped back. "Look at yourself. There isn't an unmarried man at Hawkwood who will not be vying for your attention."

Penelope couldn't see her complete form in the looking glass but what she could see made it hard to believe it was her reflection. "It doesno' look like me."

"Oh, aye it does. It looks just like you. And Thomas is going to be fighting the men to keep them away from you."

She giggled. "I doubt that, Brithwin. You have grand ideas. I hope you are no' disappointed."

"Trust me, I will not be. I cannot wait until Thomas sees you at the evening meal. He is going to fall out of his chair."

The evening meal! "Oh no, I-I canno' go oot of the room like this. Why I-I—"

"You what?" Brithwin's eyes sparkled. "You do not know what you will do with all of Thomas's attentions on you?"

The blasted heat crept up Penelope's neck and into her cheeks. She didn't have to look in the reflecting glass to know her face was as red as her hair. "I doubt very much that would be the way of things."

"Hmmm." She arched her perfectly shaped eyebrows. "Me thinks by the blush on those beautiful cheeks you like the thought."

"The truth is," Penelope looked at Brithwin, knowing she must be honest with this woman. She had been nothing but honest with her. Even if she didn't always like what she had to hear. "The truth is I dinna ken how I feel." She started pacing the floor. "My whole adult life I have had one goal. Tae be a great defender who protected my people. I have always and only looked at a man as another warrior. I have never looked at them as someone I could love or spend my life with. So this…this thing you offer me is foreign tae me. I dinna ken what tae feel or think. I ken you dinna understand, a lady like yourself."

Brithwin seemed to study her before answering. "But you are wrong, Penelope. I do understand. More than you would know. You see, I was raised by a wicked man whom I thought was my father. He enjoyed inflicting fear on me. I was very young when I decided I did not want to marry for fear a husband would be like my father. I wanted only to run my own keep and live a quiet life after he died. So I do understand your fear."

"I am no' fearful." Penelope bristled at the accusation that she was afraid of a man. She'd faced down death with many a man.

A soft smile spread across Brithwin's lips. "Perhaps fear was a poor choice of words. Apprehension might better fit. Regardless, what I want you to know is that if you give Thomas a chance you may find something you are not even looking for—like love. I cannot imagine my life without Royce in it." She let out an unladylike chortle. "And a little over a year ago I could not imagine my life with him in it!"

Penelope couldn't help but smile. And she had to admit that Brithwin had put some of her mind to ease. What could it hurt? No one could force her to marry. And Brithwin had gone to so much trouble so that she could have something else to wear. It would be inhospitable after her hostess had been so generous. "Very well. But only because you have gone tae so much work on my account."

Before she could even determine what the lady was about she was hugging her.

Chapter 9

Thomas sat on the dais with Royce, waiting for Brithwin and Penelope, listening to the pitter-patter of rain with the occasional rumble of thunder outside the window behind him.

"What is keeping those women?" Royce called out to one of the kitchen servants placing food on the table. "Are you sure they heard you when you summoned them?"

The woman looked up from her task. "Aye, milord. Milady said she would be down straight away."

"Women." Royce shook his head. "I believe Brithwin enjoys making me wait on her to arrive."

Thomas grinned, thinking back to earlier times. "I do remember a time when milady did her best to beat you to the table so she could sit in your seat."

Royce chuckled. "Aye, and now she pays me back."

"You did make it clear you would not tolerate her arriving early and taking your seat."

"And I am not sure if 'twas such a grand idea because she makes me suffer for it."

Royce had barely got the words out when he let out a low, slow whistle which brought Thomas's attention around behind him where the lord of Hawkwood gazed. Brithwin had treaded into the room and right behind her...Thomas blinked, was...Penelope?

A nudge in his side from Royce's elbow brought his attention back to the man sitting next to him.

"Might ye reconsider about a warrior wife, my friend?" A glint of humor twinkled in his eyes.

Too stunned to answer, Thomas couldn't tear his gaze off the woman who only hours before looked like a soldier. But this tall woman who still held herself like a knight could perhaps break down his resistance.

The two ladies made their way to the dais. Thomas's heart beat harder than the blacksmith's hammer as she stepped up to take her seat beside him. He nearly toppled his chair over, trying to stand up to pull out hers.

She gave him a shy smile. "Thank you, Sir Thomas."

He cleared his throat. "Call me Thomas, please."

He caught Brithwin's grin as she took her seat beside her husband. He looked away, putting his attention back on the beautiful woman beside him.

Leaning toward Penelope, he spoke in hopes that no one would hear. "You look beautiful. Blue is a lovely color for you, milady."

Her flawless cheeks turned the prettiest shade of pink. Wisps of red hair escaped beneath her braided crown, softening her features even more. He took a deep breath, willing his heart to slow. He'd faced death on the battlefield and never thought his heart would jump out of his chest. How could a woman do such a thing to him?

"You are kind tae say such nonsense." Her cheeks darkened in color, giving him hope that perhaps he affected her the same way.

"'Tis no twaddle I say. My honor rests on truthfulness." He hesitated before uttering the last words. "As well you know."

She smiled and he thought that perhaps acknowledging her status of a fighter pleased her. "Aye, 'tis the truth."

Brithwin leaned forward so she could be seen from beside the large frame of her husband. "Perhaps you could persuade Penelope to accompany you to the village on the morrow. Royce tells me you will be riding down there. Sure I am that Penelope would enjoy some time away from here."

She turned to the red-headed Scot. "Is not that so?"

The lovely lass beside him had just put a bite of meat in her mouth. Her eyes widened as she chewed the food. He could only imagine how relieved she was that she had her mouth full and couldn't answer. Instead she smiled.

Brithwin grinned. "I shall take that smile as an aye. Then it is settled, Thomas. You will take

Penelope with you on the morrow. I have some things I need to see to and knowing my new friend is in your capable hands has relieved my mind."

"With all due respect, Milady, I'm not making the trip down to the village for pleasure." Thomas looked to Royce for help. But his lord just kept his gaze on his plate as he stuffed more food into his mouth. He could see that Royce had no desire to involve himself in the machinations of his wife.

"As you know, Penelope is a feared combatant. Sure I am that she would accompany you as such if you prefer not to have a lady with you."

"Nay," Thomas replied, knowing he'd receive no help from his lord. He'd just have to make the best of Brithwin's interference. And the best was taking Penelope down to the village dressed as a lady.

"Wonderful. Then it is all settled. When would you like her ready?" Brithwin batted her lashes at him, giving him her innocent look.

He truly hated when she got the best of him. It seemed that ever since she married Royce she had honed those skills of hers.

He looked beside him to find Penelope mesmerized with her food. She probably found the conversation as awkward as he did. There was no reason to blame her for his mistress's doings. He was well aware what the lady of the manor was up to. "We will depart after we break our fast on the morrow." A loud crack jolted the heavens, followed by a bolt of lightning so brilliant it brightened the dimly lit room. "Unless of course it continues to rain."

Penelope cocked her head to the side and peeked out of the corners of her eyes. "You do not ride in the rain?"

Thomas's words caught in his throat. "A-aye I do." This woman was as bad as Brithwin with her questioning him.

"Weel, if the rain will no' harm you, sure I am that 'twill no' harm me either." Her cinnamon colored eyes bore into him.

"Do you need a chaperone, lass? I would not want to sully your reputation." Thomas hoped that would put an end to this.

"'Tis sure I am that me reputation would no' be sullied by visiting the village."

Thomas let out a sigh. He knew when he'd been defeated.

†††

A light tug sent the tunic over Penelope's head, and with haste she pushed her arms through the sleeve holes. The last thing she wanted was to be late, giving Thomas a reason to go without her. 'Twas true what Brithwin said, she could not wait to get on a horse and feel the wind in her hair.

Tap-tap-tap. The sound came from the heavy wooden door. Brithwin pushed it open and peeked in. "Just checking on your progress this morn—" She cut her words short and sailed into the room. "Nay, nay. You cannot go like that."

Penelope frowned as she looked on her new friend. "Like what?"

"Weel," she sashayed up to her and grasped

Penelope's hands. "Like a knight of course. I have known Thomas a very long time and I have never seen him quite so taken with a lady. But you need to remind him that you *are* a lady as well as a warrior."

"I dinna ken. I feel I am trying tae be someone I am no'."

Brithwin's brows shot up. "You are saying you are no lady?" She squeezed Penelope's hands.

Not really knowing how to answer that question, Penelope gazed down at their clasped hands. Heaven's above. She had been a soldier for so many years, yesterday was like a dream—a dream that would always be out of her reach. Up until she'd met Brithwin and Thomas she'd never longed to marry. She'd been content with her decision. But seeing Brithwin with her husband and the happiness they shared made her realize her life was missing something.

And Thomas, what was it about the man who drew her to him?

A gentle squeeze of her hands brought her attention back to Brithwin. "Sorry I am. I became lost in my thoughts. What did you ask?"

"I asked you if you cannot see how much of a lady you are. Why men will be falling at your feet wanting to spend time with you."

Penelope couldn't hold back the laughter. Such nonsense. "'Tis sure I am as you are before me that I need not worry myself with that problem."

Brithwin let go of her hands and nearly floated across the floor with her elegance. Scooping up the gown Penelope had worn the previous day, the lady of the manor made her way back before Penelope.

With no trouble at all, Brithwin pulled Penelope's tunic from her head, tossed it aside and made much quicker work at putting on the chemise, kirtle, and surcoat. Brithwin worked with such efficiency that Penelope didn't say a word for fear she'd disturb her.

Brithwin pointed to the chair where Penelope obediently sat, and handed her stockings and garters to her. Penelope put on the stockings and shoes with no argument. She had a feeling that it wouldn't help anyway. Brithwin would have her way when she wanted it, that she was sure. She'd just finished fastening her shoes when Brithwin untied the braid Penelope had finished just before struggling to get in her tunic.

"I shall return with haste." Brithwin rushed out of the room and returned with a comb and circlet. "It never hurts to make a man wait for you. 'Tis not good to make them think you are anxious to see them."

Penelope once again resigned herself to Brithwin's wishes. The thin tines cut through her red curly locks. "Seems like a silly game tae me. I have no' the patience for such things. 'Tis why this is such a bad idea. I will never truly be a lady. I dinna have the sophistication. I gave that up when I chose tae be a protector of my people."

"Ach! 'Tis because of those things you draw Thomas's eye. I never want to hear you say you are no lady." Brithwin pulled her up and held the small looking glass before her. "Look at that beautiful creature staring back at you and tell me she is not a lady."

"But I dinna ken the right things tae say. I am so awkward around him." Penelope paused and turned to Brithwin, her unruly hair even more out of control, released from the braid. "You are very guid at what you do, milady."

"And what prithee do I do?"

"You have me dressing up and going on a ride with a man with other ideas than being a soldier."

"But I could see the interest you had in him. 'Twas not me who put the desire for Thomas in your heart. I, my dear, am only cultivating it. Helping you come out from behind your sword and bow."

Penelope laughed. "You may feign innocence, Lady Brithwin, I may hide behind my weapons, but I see how well you wield your sword—your matchmaker's sword that is."

Chapter 10

A sudden melancholy came over Penelope's friend. "I hope I dinna offend you, Brithwin."

She smiled, but there was sadness in it. "Nay, no offense was taken."

"What has caused you tae become sullen?" Penelope sat back down to allow Brithwin to finish taming her hair.

As Brithwin parted her hair down the back and began to braid she drew in a breath. "I do not want you to leave. You have become my friend."

The words warmed Penelope's heart. "'Tis guid tae hear you say such things. I have no' had many friends in my life."

"I see many similarities between you and me."

"Oh?" The two were night and day. Penelope couldn't think of one thing they had in common.

"I've had few friends myself. And you lost your father and your people and I know that leaves you feeling alone. I grew up with a man who I believed was my father and though I was surrounded by people who loved me and protected me many times without me knowing, I still felt alone. When the man I believed was my father would punish me I almost felt despair. But I had one thing you do not. I had the Lord. I could not have walked that road without Him."

A knot began to form in the pit of Penelope's stomach. "Glad I am that you found comfort in your God. I ken He answers some people's prayers. Mine he does no'."

"Oh, He answers everyone's prayers. Just not the way we may want. If He had answered my prayers like I wanted I would not be here at Hawkwood. For there were times when I was younger, I prayed God to take me away from Hawkwood, and that I never would have to return. And more recently if He had answered my prayers as I asked, Royce would not be my husband. I shudder to think what would have happened to him. I did not wish very nice things on him." She smiled.

"Things dinna turn out good for everyone. If it did my da' would be alive as weel as my people."

"But God still hears you and cares for you. If He did not, He would not have sent you here to Hawkwood to me—and to Thomas."

The early morning heat filled the small room. Penelope leaned forward and scooped a fan off the small table and began to cool herself. "I have had tae many disappointments. I shall no' get my hopes up."

"And we know that all things work together for good to them who love God, to them who are the called according to His purpose." Brithwin paused as she arranged the circlet on Penelope's head. "It's a scripture from the Bible. It is in the book of Romans."

"I see." Penelope didn't really know what to say. Although she was impressed that Brithwin knew scriptures well enough to repeat.

"It is a promise from God. If you are His, He will take whatever Satan means for bad and turn it to good."

†††

Never had she been so ready to head down to break her fast. The conversation had gotten much too serious for her. Brithwin put the final touch on her hair and Penelope headed toward the door exclaiming how famished she was.

The morning meal turned out just as heavy as Brithwin's and her talk. Thomas arrived in a rather foul mood. She imagined it was because he had to drag her along. She almost bowed out from going but she wanted to get away so badly she didn't give in to Thomas's brooding. And then when she slung on her bow and quiver of arrows, she could see Brithwin's disappointment. The only one who did not seem bothered by anything was Royce.

She threw herself onto the mahogany bay palfrey they'd readied for her. Brithwin looked as if she would faint, for she had refused to ride side saddle. The gown did have some extra fabric to cover her legs. Still it was not very ladily. But then up until the last sennight or so she'd always considered herself as only a soldier. But it was quite clear they did not. It was nearly an insult for her to ride a palfrey. They'd not put a knight on one.

Once on their way, she smiled as she remembered Brithwin's shock when she'd thrown herself onto the horse. It was obvious Thomas was none too happy to have to bring her along. She shrugged to herself. It appeared no one was pleased with her today.

And why Brithwin believed the man was interested in her, Penelope would never know. She would have to put her foot down the next time Brithwin tried to throw them together.

Glancing at the man beside her, she decided he could never be accused of being a loquacious person. But that could easily have to do with the fact that he was not happy about the situation. Ah well, she was going to enjoy her trip regardless. It was nice to look around and not see walls in every direction.

"What makes you smile, lass?" Thomas looked on her with head cocked.

"I am glad tae be oot of the castle walls."

"And…" He didn't take his eyes from her.

Growing up around boys and spending her time with them, she'd never learned the art of being coy. At the moment she regretted that.

"I see it on the tip of your tongue, lass. Out with it." He almost seemed amused.

That gave her the courage she needed. "I was thinking of the look on Brithwin's face when I mounted my horse with bow and quiver. She seemed a bit—"

"Appalled?" He grinned at her. "Do not let her trouble you, lass. There was many a time that our sweet Brithwin looked as if she were a peasant. As a matter of fact, Royce thought she was a servant the first time he met her. She had been working in her flowers and was covered in dirt from head to toe." Thomas let out a chortle. "He was none too happy when he discovered he had mistaken his future wife for a serving wench."

She cocked her head. "Are you inferring that I look like a peasant?"

"Do not twist my words, lass. 'Tis no wonder you and Brithwin get along so well. You have much in common."

✝✝✝

Thomas could live the rest of his life listening to the tinkling laughter that spilled from deep within Penelope. The woman had captured his heart without even trying. When he saw her dressed as a woman should, it nearly stole his breath away as a cat will steal the breath of a sleeping babe.

But he could not marry a fighter and though Penelope was dressed as a lady today, she also brought along her bow and quiver of arrows. And he could not help but notice she rode her horse astride.

A slight giggle remained in her voice as she replied. "I, sir, have no idea of which you speak. However, I will confess that I am a quick study."

"I would not doubt that." Thomas said under his breath.

"For what are we coming to the village?"

Penelope inquired.

"Either Royce or I come and talk to the people. We like to make sure there have been no problems from outsiders."

"You mean Scotsmen?"

"Aye, Scotsmen and Englishmen. Any who do not belong here. 'Tis the way we keep the people safe. If a stranger arrives, we talk to them. Find out what their business is, how long they are staying, those kinds of things."

"Ah. Like you did with me?"

"Aye." He reined his horse past a wooded area as they continued toward the village. The town people had been quiet. That was usually a good sign that life was going along as it should. Royce had asked him to make this trip to town. Thomas shook his head. He had to wonder if Brithwin had put him up to it.

They spent the morning talking with the people. A few had seen strangers but none who had stayed on or seemed to cause any problems. The village was small and most everyone knew each other. Thomas made his way down to the cottage of Mary, the old healer. He rapped on the door of her house.

"Ye dinna have to bang the door down." Her voice rang out through the cloth covering the window.

Thomas shrugged at Penelope. "I thought she was hard of hearing."

Penelope smiled. "Apparently, she is no'."

The door creaked open and he peered into the prunish face of the old woman. The white-haired matron looked older every time he saw her. "Good day, Mary."

She gave him a toothless smile when she saw him. "Good day to ye Sir Thomas. I thought ye'd be those kids."

"The kids not be giving you trouble, are they?" He'd have a word with them if they were.

She flicked her hand in the air. "They only be doing what you probably did as a boy—and they make me get out of me chair. 'Tis good for me bones. Come on in and tell me how the lord and lady be."

Thomas stepped back and Penelope maneuvered around the old door and into the cottage.

"Who do ye have here, Sir Thomas? Did ye finally find yerself a wife?"

Penelope stepped forward and curtsied. "Guid day tae you, Mary. I am Penelope. The daughter of a friend of Thomas's father."

The old woman scratched her head. "I have to think about that."

Thomas slid in beside Penelope. "No, she is not my wife. Her father and my father were…acquaintances."

"That doesno' surprise me. I think yer too ornery to marry."

Penelope let out a giggle that caused Thomas to smile.

"So, what brings ye here, my boy. Sure I am that it is no' to see an old woman."

Thomas ducked his head. "Brithwin asked me to bring back some herbs."

She let out a cackle. "'Tis no hard feelings boy. I see ye have much better things to do with yer time. What is it my lady would like?"

"Horehound, comfrey, yarrow…" he continued with Brithwin's list that he'd memorized.

She shuffled toward a table piled with bottles, baskets, and cloths. "Slow down, son. I am an old woman and can no' move that fast. Now you said comfrey and horehound. Where did I put those?"

By the time she'd gathered what Brithwin had asked for, the morning was all but gone. Thomas thanked the healer as he put a coin in her hand and left. The day had gotten away from him. He supposed it was because of the beautiful woman with him.

They mounted their horses and left the village behind.

"Your people, they are vera kind."

Thomas kept his eyes on the road ahead. "Most of them are."

"They think highly of your laird and lady."

"Aye. Royce and Brithwin are fair. They are good to everyone."

"Even me."

That got Thomas's attention. "Why wouldn't they be?"

She shrugged causing the bow slung over her back and shoulder to wobble. "There is much tension on our borders."

"But you did not come to steal or pillage."

Her face lit up with a smile. "Nay, I dinna. I came tae find your da."

Thomas knew he was weakening as he stared into her beautiful cinnamon eyes that lit up when she smiled. He wanted to reach out and drag her onto his mount and kiss her flawless lips.

It was the crack of a branch that snapped him out of his woolgathering. Before he saw them he had his sword pulled out of its scabbard at the ready. "Go to Hawkwood!" He yelled over his shoulder as two men on horseback emerged from the woods.

"Nay! I can help." Penelope had pulled her bow from her back and nocked an arrow as her horse jigged beneath her.

"Go! Now!" What was wrong with the woman?

He turned back just as the riders were on him. Metal clanged against metal when the swords met and the rider passed him by. He raised his sword again, this time to deflect the second rider's attack. Spinning his horse's hind quarters around he faced his first attacker again. The brute raised his sword and charged. Thomas again deflected the sharp blade. Kicking Wife in the sides he moved his horse in a tight circle to come back and meet the first attacker.

The metal of their weapons rang in the air over and over as they hit together. He could see his opponent tiring and he pressed him back until the second man came in at a charge. Thomas had little time to think as the second bore down with sword raised. He swung in an arc as the man came up beside him, and landed the sword on the man's neck. He tumbled to the ground.

Where was Penelope? Had she done as she was told? In the heat of the battle he'd forgotten her. He swung around, his eyes scanning while the horse danced beneath him. The daft woman hadn't moved. But she had her bow pulled back, an arrow nocked, and it pointed straight at him.

Chapter 11

Penelope opened her mouth to warn Thomas of the man behind him but the words caught in her throat. It was as if she watched the death of her father all over. Thomas locked eyes with her. The words wouldn't come, so she released the arrow from her bow and watched it split through the air and meet its target. The enemy dropped his sword and it tumbled to the ground with a harmless thud as he grabbed the arrow that penetrated his chest. In a few seconds he followed the way of his weapon.

The anger in Thomas's eyes might do her more harm than the two men charging out of the woods and toward the riderless horses. Thomas dug his heals into his mount and charged at her. As his horse sped alongside, he leaned out and slapped the palfrey's hind quarter. The animal let out a snort and dug its hooves into the dirt.

The poor horse probably hadn't run that fast in years. She glanced back to see if Thomas had followed but the stubborn man had spun back around and now chased the two men who had managed to mount onto one horse. The other horse, still riderless, quickly gained on her.

Penelope slowed the bay she rode, slipped her arm and head through her bow and her quiver strap just in time to lean out as the black horse passed, snatching the dangling reins of the spooked animal. He submitted to the pressure of the bridle and trotted alongside her.

She loathed doing it but the memory of Thomas's anger along with knowing that it was because of her that he almost lost his life, she sped toward Hawkwood to send help. She flew through the open portcullis, through the outer ward and gate house to the bailey.

Slowing her horse as she drew near a group of men, she jumped from her horse before it stopped and nearly fell flat on her face, forgetting she wore a lady's gown.

Jarren, alert that something was wrong, grabbed her arm to steady her. "What is amiss?"

She found herself out of breath. "We-we were ambushed. Outside the village. Thomas-Thomas needs help."

Jarren threw himself on the black stallion she'd just brought in and raced out the gate. The others ran to the stables and followed.

Helplessness filled her. The defender in her wanted to follow, but Thomas's anger burned in her memory. Tears welled in her eyes from frustration. She didn't like this feeling of being powerless. She wanted to fight—to vent out the turmoil inside her.

And then a voice inside her repeated the words of Brithwin, "God still hears you and cares for you." Penelope hadn't said a prayer since she was a child, but prayer was all she had.

"God, if Brithwin is right and you do hear me and care, then show me you are real and you still love me. Bring Thomas home safely."

She looked up toward the heavens. Somewhere in the back of her mind she'd heard you shouldn't put conditions on God. But she had to promise Him something if He would rescue Thomas. "If You do, I promise never tae doubt You again."

With his long stride, Royce made his way down the keep steps, taking two at a time. "What is the commotion about?" He looked to the men riding out of the keep as if the castle walls were caving in on them.

"We were ambushed not tae far from the village." She was relieved that her voice was now controlled and steady. More of a warrior.

"How many?" Royce stared off toward the men riding out the gates.

"Four, but only two survived unscathed. Two are wounded or worse."

She saw Royce's shoulders drop as they relaxed. "Thomas will bring them in." He scratched his cheek. "Although I am surprised that so many of my men went to help."

That dreadful blush crept back up Penelope's cheeks and she willed the heat away. "I may have forgotten tae mention how many." What was happening to her? She never forgot such things.

Royce grinned. "No harm done. The men have been bored lately. Gives them something to occupy their minds."

"Come, let us find Brithwin. She would not be pleased with me should I not inform her of this turn of events. She thinks highly of you."

His hand barely brushed the small of her back and though she didn't look, she had the feeling he held it there in case she were to collapse. She sighed inwardly. No one would believe her a true soldier after this. Other than when her father was killed, never had she felt so much fear. When the men had emerged from the woods she was ready to face death. But to watch Thomas fall to the sword…she could not bear such pain.

Once up the steps and in the keep, Royce apparently trusted her legs not to give out as he moved ahead, calling out to Brithwin.

The lady of the keep glided across the great hall floor. "I was just coming to see what all the noise was about." She rushed to Penelope and took her hands. "Did something happen? Are you injured?"

"She is fine, Brithwin. Just a small skirmish." Royce leaned down and kissed his wife's forehead before heading out from whence he came.

She smiled at Brithwin to reassure her.

Brithwin kept her eyes on her retreating husband and shook her head. "What happened? Wait. Let us go sit in my solar."

When they made it to the solar, Brithwin poured them each a glass of water. "Now, tell me what happened. Where is Thomas?"

"I nearly caused Thomas his life."

Brithwin smiled. "But you did not."

"Nay. Weel I do hope no'. We were ambushed on our way back from the village. Thomas told me tae go tae Hawkwood. But I could no' ride away and leave him tae fight the two men on his own. I had tae stay for fear he would need my help. He turned and saw that I had no' moved from where he left me. The anger that blazed in his eyes was unforgettable. It is etched in my memory for eternity. One of the Scotsman came up from behind. I had already had my arrow nocked in case he needed my help. I let the arrow go and shot the man. Thomas took care of the other. Then two more came from the woods on foot. They mounted one horse and Thomas chased after them." She sniffed and tried to hold back the tears burning in her eyes but one and then another fell.

"It will be fine, my friend. It sounds to me like you saved Thomas's life." Brithwin leaned up in her chair and patted Penelope's hand.

"Aye, after I almost got him killed." More tears spilled down her face. "And I dinna cry! These tears seem insistent on falling."

Brithwin soothed. "Maybe you cry because you love the man and you thought you might lose him."

Penelope used the long loose fabric from her sleeve to dab her eyes. She sniffed. "I dinna have him tae lose."

Brithwin gave her a knowing smile. "Oh, but I think you do."

†††

Thomas shoved the two men down on their knees in front of Royce in the great hall. "These are two of the men who tried to kill our guest and myself. Tam and Hendrie. They claim they do not know much about the other two." They were young, barely able to grow hair on their face. And the younger one with bright red hair trembled so severely he could scarcely stay upon his knees. The other couldn't have been more than a few years older.

"Who sent you to kill our guest? I take that as a personal insult. My guests should feel safe when they come here." Royce stood with his feet braced apart and his arms crossed in front of him.

"No one was supposed tae get killed." The older of the two answered.

Thomas raised his brows. "Is that so?"

The younger elbowed the older. "Tell 'em."

"Nay," the other said. "They 'ill kill us if they are no' already dead."

The younger, still quivering, nodded toward Royce and Thomas. "Well if you dinna, they will. We got a better chance here."

"Who are the others you speak of?" Royce asked.

There was a moment of silence. Thomas almost groaned thinking they would have to persuade them to talk.

"Tell me about the two who were with you." Thomas inquired cautiously.

"A-A rival clan." The young man answered.

"What did they want with us?" Thomas glared

down at him.

"N-Not y-you. They wanted the lass."

"Why?" Thomas could barely keep his anger in.

The older elbowed the one talking and then wagged his head back and forth.

Thomas leaned forward. "Ignore him. You have more to fear from me."

"She 'as got something they want."

"You 'ave said enough. Yer going tae get us killed." The older bemoaned.

"I will take my chances."

Thomas had to give the young man some credit for standing up to his friend. "What does she have that they want?"

"An heirloom her da gave her when he died—a cross."

Thomas had the two men taken to be locked up.

Royce walked to the great hall window that looked out over the bailey and beyond. "That cross must be worth a large sum of money for them to come this far for it."

He nodded in agreement. "Aye, perhaps a king's ransom, or maybe better said a chieftain's ransom."

Penelope and Brithwin entered the room and Penelope rushed toward him. "You have returned. And you are well?"

He smiled. Her concern pleased him. "'Twas not a problem bringing them back. They were more boys than men. They did not even carry weapons on them." He didn't tell her their weapons were most likely confiscated by the rival clan.

"I passed Hendrie and Tam on the way in. Was

it them who were with the men who attacked us?" Penelope's color left her face, leaving her pale.

"Aye, 'twas them. You know them?" Thomas grasped her shoulders to steady her. She'd been through much this day.

"Aye, I ken them. They were from my clan. I thought Tam was my friend."

His heart hurt hearing the pain of betrayal in her voice. "'Tis sorry I am."

Royce took Brithwin's hand and whispered something to her and moved her in the direction of the door. He passed by Thomas and in a low voice that Thomas barely heard, spoke to his ears alone. "God knows best when it comes to our women. 'Tis best to leave them to Him and trust in His guidance." With that he guided his wife out the door leaving him alone with Penelope.

He wanted to cheer her, to make her laugh or even smile. And as much as he didn't like her being a warrior, he wanted to see the worry vanish from her brow. "I must say you are a much better aim with your arrow than I am with my sword. I was relieved when I was not your mark."

"I do hope your Laird is no' unhappy with me."

"Nay, he left to allow us to talk in private."

She looked so lost. This had to be the first time she'd been betrayed by someone she knew and trusted. If only he could take the hurt away.

"I dinna think I ken the two men who attacked you. They dinna look familiar tae me."

Three little lines appeared between her eyebrows as she spoke. Then as if it had suddenly registered what he'd said only moments before, the lines melted away and a small smile played on her lips. "Dinna I tell you I am a better shot than most men?"

He chuckled. "That you did, Lass, that you did."

But as quickly as the smile appeared it disappeared. "Did you speak with them, Tam and Hendrie?" She shuffled her feet and glanced toward the window.

"Aye we did. The one you call Tam was rather free with his words. If he tells the truth, they were forced to bring the others."

"I can no' believe it still. A protector should be willing tae lay down his life for another."

Hurt shone in her eyes. He held his tongue. Likely they did not see her as a warrior but like him, a woman. "Tam tells a tale that these men are in search of a cross your father gave you."

She walked over to one of the chairs that faced the great hearth and sat down. He followed her over and took a chair near her.

She clasped her hands in her lap and kept her eyes focused on them. "'Tis true I am afraid. And they will no' stop until they get it."

"The cross must be very valuable for them to come this far."

"'Tis, but no' in the way you think, though the cross itself has value. But the holder of the cross is believed tae have the rights tae be a clan's chieftain if it is given tae them."

Could things get any worse? She was not only a warrior—and after today he knew he could not have a warrior as a wife, for he could not live day to day worrying about her safety. It almost cost him his life today—but now she is to be her clan's chieftain besides? "So you will return to your people and be chief?"

Chapter 12

Penelope grunted. "A woman? Nay, the cross does me nay good."

"Why would your father give it to you if it is of no benefit?"

She lifted her head and met his gaze. "Tae keep it oot of the wrong hands."

Thomas's brows wrinkled. "I am afraid I do not understand.

"Is there some place we can go?" Her gaze swept the large great hall where servants passed in and out. "Some place private where we can talk?"

"Come." He took her by the elbow and guided her up the stairs and down a long corridor, passing several sealed rooms as they went. He stopped before a large tapestry that reached to the floor. He pulled back the wall hanging with one arm and welcomed her in with the other. The wall recessed behind the tapestry and a small padded bench sat under a window.

She lowered herself onto the seat. His leg brushed hers as he sat. Her senses heightened. She'd put herself into a compromising situation. Should anyone come upon them…

Thomas must have read her thoughts. "Concern yourself not that someone will find us. This corridor is Royce and Brithwin's private sleeping quarters and solar. No one will happen on us here."

Aye, they were in the laird and lady's wing for she'd just been to Brithwin's solar. "I would no' want tae give people the wrong impression."

He paused for a moment, not taking his eyes off her. "But if you have gone to battle with all men, why would you worry about your honor?"

She lifted her chin. "My father always accompanied me as my chaperone." The pain of her father's death struck her like it only yesterday he had died rather than the many months that had passed.

"I do not mean to insult you, lass. I only asked."

The words did more than insult her. They hurt. There were many names and accusations hurled her way as a soldier and because of that she tried her best not to let words wound her. But coming from Thomas, they cut as the blade of a sword slicing the skin but she would never allow him to know.

"What is it you wish to tell me that you wish not others to hear?" Thomas asked.

She only meant to tell Thomas about the cross and why her father gave it to her. Instead, her words spilled forth and she told him her life from the time she'd chosen to become a defender of her people until he found her at Hawkwood.

"See you now, by me having the cross, any man with ambitions of being a chieftain or wanting blessings on their clan would marry me. 'Twas my father's way of making sure I would find a husband. What he dinna think aboot on his death bed was the danger it would put me in as well. Though it has tae be given, not all believe the same. I could give it for my ransom, some would say."

"If most of your clan died by the MacAlister's hand, who is left for you to marry?"

†††

Thomas reached out and took her hand to comfort her when tears welled in her eyes. Ach! He was no good at courting. He was too old for it. Courtly love was for young men. He said the wrong things. First, he insulted her and now he'd made her cry. The woman would never be interested in him. His chest had ached so much for this woman. Even Brithwin, who he loved like a daughter, didn't affect his whole being like this beautiful creature did. He was full of advice for Brithwin and never had trouble saying the right thing. If this was what love did, he wasn't sure he wanted any part of it. But he wasn't sure he could live without Penelope's now that she had gotten hold of his heart.

"That did not come out as it should have, lass. Any man would be a fool not to want to marry you."

She looked at him with what he could only call an attempt at a smile. But the tear trailing down her cheek told the truth of how he'd hurt her. "I ken what you meant. Please don't fash yourself aboot it. There is no' many men left in my clan. Two of which you have under your guard. But I dinna think they are a suitable match for me since they were my betrayers."

"Nay, they are not worthy of you lass."

"Truly, I dinna think that Tam saw my da give me the cross. But he is the only one who was close by when me da passed."

"If your father kept the cross with him and you were the last to be with your father, 'twould not take much to figure out who he had given it to."

"'Tis no' just my clan who will want this cross. There are clans who believe the same thing, that the cross brings blessings on the chieftain and his people."

"It did not help your father or your people."

"Nay, I see that it was a silly superstition that we put our trust in."

He rubbed his thumb across the smooth skin on the back of her hand, and couldn't help but notice the palm of her hand was much like the skin of his mistress. A hand that was not afraid of work. "Surely the others will see this also and not seek after you."

Her gaze lowered to where he caressed her hand. "They will find a way tae dismiss it. They will say me da was undeserving of the honor or some other rubbish. Aye, they will seek me out."

"You cannot be forced to marry." He wanted to encourage her, to take away the sadness he heard in her voice.

Her lips quivered into a smile. "Like Brithwin was no' forced into marriage?"

That gave him pause. He had been a strong influence on his mistress marrying Royce. Going as far as sending a missive to the king asking for his blessing and telling him the union was welcomed by both parties. It took much persuasion to convince her marrying Royce was in her people's best interest. "It was best for Brithwin. I knew that Royce would be good to her and he would take care with her."

"So you are saying she was no' forced? Aye, she said the words willing tae marry the man, but only because she was led tae believe there was no other way."

"But she loves Royce and he loves her."

"'Tis true she told me so herself. But that is no' the case for all, Thomas. I am no fool tae believe I will marry for love. I will more likely than no' marry tae save what remains of my people."

Thomas's heart sprang into action before his brain could tell his mouth to stop. "I would marry you lass."

Her head shot up and she met his gaze. "You would marry me as I am?"

Thomas lowered his head and gently brushed his lips over hers, sending an urgent fire through his veins.

"Lass, there is nothing I would want to change about you."

He saw hope spring into her eyes.

"No' even being a warrior?"

"If you are married to me you need not fight. You would be a wife." When the words left his mouth, he knew it was not the words she wanted to hear. For her smile faded as she turned her head and stared out the window.

She stood. "I have wasted enough of your time, Thomas. Sure I am that you have men who need you."

She rushed out before he got to his feet. He'd made a mess of things. But he could not marry a woman who insisted on fighting battles beside him. Today had shown him that. The woman would get him killed because he could not keep his mind on the fight. And if the enemy did not kill him, Royce would for he would be useless worrying about Penelope. Why did he ever let his heart become involved with a woman? He shoved himself to his feet and growled. "Brithwin!"

†††

For the first time in Penelope's life she didn't feel like the fierce avenger she had chosen to be for her people. But neither did she feel like a woman. What she did feel like was the little girl she was never really allowed to be. Her feet wouldn't take her fast enough to her room. Though she wanted to look behind her to see if Thomas followed, she willed herself not to.

She went to her room and removed her gown and replaced it with the clothes in which she'd arrived at Hawkwood. She lay on the bed and gave herself permission to cry, something she rarely did, yet here she was crying a second time today. But in her room with no men, no knights, no father, she afforded herself the luxury.

With her pillow damp, she rolled onto her back and tried not to think about Thomas. She found that impossible as she asked herself what kind of fighter was he? When the tears were gone, she fumed at herself for allowing the weakness. It helped naught.

Birds chirped outside her window and children's laughter floated in from the courtyard that her window faced. A colorful bouquet of flowers sat on the small table in her room. Brithwin must have put them there for her.

She'd missed the nooning meal but wasn't hungry even as the evening mealtime crept up on her. A light tapping on the door brought her off the bed. "Aye?"

"'Tis me, Brithwin."

"Come in." Penelope went to the chair and sat as Brithwin came in the room. "Please come and sit with me."

There was no denying the surprise on Brithwin's face when she saw Penelope in her own clothes. Her friend said nothing, but she didn't have to because the look on her face said it all.

Brithwin sat beside her. "Are you ill?"

"Perhaps in heart." She attempted a smile but knew it was half-hearted.

"'Tis Thomas then. I thought as much. The man has been ornery as a wild boar. I do not mean to pry..."

Penelope couldn't help but to smile. "Aye, you do."

Brithwin let out a giggle. "I am afraid so—especially when it concerns two people I have come to love very much."

Penelope swallowed the lump that popped up in her throat. Other than her father, she never remembered anyone saying they loved her. "You have become like a sister tae me. 'Tis nice tae have had another female tae talk tae."

Brithwin narrowed her eyes. "You speak as if this is coming to an end."

"I am afraid it is. My heart canno' take the pain. I must face my future and that is in Scotland. I do thank you for your hospitality, Brithwin. And your friendship. It has meant more tae me than you will ever know."

"No, you do not need to leave. Whatever happened between you and Thomas can be worked out. I could tell you stories of Royce and I. Why, it seemed that there was no way we could be happy."

Penelope reached across the small table with the flowers on it and grasped her friend's hand. "You have been a real sister to me. And I will never forget that. But I tell you the truth, this morning I prayed my first prayer since I can scarcely remember. I prayed Thomas would no' die but that God would protect him. And now, now my heart has broken like a piece of glass."

Brithwin put her other hand on Penelope's. "There was a time I thought to run away from Royce. I did not think I could bear it here any longer. But deep in my soul, the Lord nudged me to stay. Oh, I wanted to run and run far. But I knew if I did…well, that is of no concern right now. Make sure you are not running from something God has for you. Because I promise you, His way is always the best." She paused for a moment and looked to be in thought. "I will say no more after this because this must be your decision, but it seems to me if you prayed and God answered your prayer, it is only fair that you see what He has in store for you."

True to her word, Brithwin never said another word about it. She quietly rose. "Will you be at the evening meal?"

Penelope gave her what she was sure was a halfhearted smile. "I dinna think I will this evening." She didn't want to face Thomas.

Chapter 13

Thomas sat at the table breaking his fast, watching for Penelope. He'd missed her at the meal yestereve. Though Royce was younger, the man had wisdom, especially when it came to women. Perhaps, Royce was right about trusting their women to God. But Penelope wasn't his—not yet.

Most of the men had finished eating and had left the great hall, including Royce. Brithwin sat and rolled a strawberry around on her plate with the tip of her knife, deep in thought.

Attempting to take his mind off the Scottish lass, he turned to Brithwin. "What is on your mind, Brithwin? You are quiet this morn."

She let out a heavy sigh. "I am feeling rather sad today, Thomas. I miss my friend."

Alarm shot through Thomas's body. "Are we speaking of Penelope?"

She looked up at him with what he thought could be a wee bit of impatience. "How many friends do I have here at Hawkwood, Thomas?"

Thomas thought. Elspeth, though her servant was also her friend, but she had gone to take care of family. She spoke of Penelope.

"Is she leaving?" He tightened his hands into fists, awaiting her response.

She looked him in the eye, and he saw anger. "Oh nay, she is not leaving."

Relief rushed over him like cool water on a hot day. He could not understand the anger he heard in her voice as well as saw in her eyes. "Then what troubles you?"

"She has already left." Brithwin lifted her chin and the picture of Penelope lifting her chin when he had insulted her flashed through his mind.

He stood up abruptly, sending the chair falling back and off the dais. "Where did she go?"

"I would think back from whence she came." Brithwin exhaled with force as if he'd asked a silly question.

"When did she leave?" Urgency built inside him.

"I do not know. She was gone when I went to check on her this morning. The last time I spoke with her was before the evening repast." Her anger seemed to disappear and she sniffed.

"Did she say anything that made you think she was returning to Scotland?"

"Only that she must go and face her future." She sniffed again. "I had hoped her future would be here at Hawkwood."

"By the rood! Did you not think this information was something I would like to know, Brithwin?"

Royce walked into the great hall as Thomas swung around and stepped off the dais. "Is there a reason you raise your voice at my wife, Thomas?"

Thomas stormed past his lord and friend. "Ask your wife. Perhaps she will be more forthcoming with you than she has been with me."

†††

Brithwin stood and smiled as Thomas stormed out of the hall.

Royce grasped his wife by the waist and swung her down from the platform. "Wife, why are you looking like the man who just stole the king's crown?"

"Oh, no reason, husband. 'Tis a lovely summer's day. Did you miss me so much that you had to come see me again?"

Royce let out a loud chuckle. "Will I be in as much trouble as my master-at-arms if I tell you nay?"

She gave him a sassy smile and threw her arms around his neck. "Nay, I think not. I do believe things are going to work out just fine. So why did you return so soon? I thought you had work to see to."

Royce let out a sigh. "I came to speak with the man you seemed to have chased off."

Brithwin grinned. "Well dear husband, you might want to get Jarren to help you with what you need. If my guess is correct, you will not be seeing Thomas for a wee bit."

"And where do you think the man will be going, my love?"

"Oh, if I were to guess, I would say to Scotland to track down a young lass who caught his eye."

Royce squeezed her. "Now, do you think that after yesterday morning that is a good idea? The man cannot go riding into another country alone."

"I never thought of that." She looked up at him and gave him her biggest smile. "So I guess you will have to send some of your men along as escorts."

Royce bent his head and brushed his lips over hers. "Me is beginning to think I need to take Thomas's advice and have a talk with me wife."

†††

Thomas was furious with Brithwin. After gathering supplies, he stomped out to the stables and readied Wife. The destrier danced beneath him feeling the tension that simmered in Thomas. He had no real idea where to find Penelope. Scotland was a large country. But she found Hawkwood on foot so surely, he could find her on a mount. And he knew she came from the highlands. That was a start. Someone would know where her clan resided.

As he sat for a moment securing his pack he glanced up and out the portcullis. She could be on foot or taken one of the horses. It would be much better for his search to know how she traveled. He climbed off Wife and went into the stables and found the stable master.

"Are any horses missing?"

"Nay."

"The Scottish lass, did she borrow a horse this morning?"

"Nay. We even have an extra. The black you brought in yesterday."

Thomas nodded to the man and made it to the doorway when he stopped. He'd intended on giving that horse to Penelope—her spoils of battle. Perhaps he should bring the beast with him. Could be a peace offering.

"Put a halter on the new black. I will be taking him with me." He waited for the stable master to bring him the horse.

He admired the animal as it moved toward him. It was a fine horse. Anyone would be happy to own the beast. Thomas accepted the rope from the stable master and started leading the black out when he was nearly run over by knights hurrying to their mounts.

"Where to are you, men headed?" Thomas stopped and asked no one in particular.

"Royce has sent us on a mission." Adam answered.

"Is that so?"

"Aye, he tells us we are to ride with you."

Thomas welcomed the men. His job would be much easier and much less dangerous with a group. "I will wait out front for you."

He led the black to where he had left Wife and tied its lead to his saddle. When the men were all saddled up, the group made their way out of the bailey and through the gates.

Adam trotted his horse up beside him. "What is the mission, Thomas?"

"Royce did not tell you?"

"Nay, he told us there was no time and to ready our horses. You would explain what was needed."

"We head north to bring back Lady Penelope." Thomas planned to leave it at that.

"The warrior woman?" Adam asked.

He wasn't sure why that question irritated him so much. He supposed because he didn't want other men thinking of her as a warrior. "Her name is Penelope."

Adam let out a low whistle. "I see why Royce sent us. I would not want to face down that woman alone. Have you seen her with her bow or her knife? Why I do not believe there is a man in Royce's service who could hit a target better than that lass."

Thomas did his best not to seem surprised by the man's observation. "And you know that how?"

"I thought surely she would tell you."

"Apparently not everyone has been privy to that information so do explain yourself." Thomas didn't keep the irritation from his voice as well as he'd hoped to.

"Elfed challenged her. Told her if she won he would give her his sword. If he won she had to forfeit her bow and knife."

"I guess I do not need to ask who won, since she had her bow last I saw her."

Adam rumbled with laughter. "Nay, you need not ask. The lass beat him twice. 'Twas a fair challenge, too. She hit the target center every time with her arrow."

"So Elfed no longer owns a sword? He will not be much help on the battlefield without one."

Thomas grinned. That had to be humiliating to the man.

"Nay, Elfed has his weapon. The lass would not take it. She said she had no need for it."

The lass is as honorable as any knight he served with and more honorable than some, Elfed included. The man had hoped to embarrass Penelope. Thomas was pleased that he had failed.

Adam nodded toward the horse. "And the black?"

"A peace offering." Thomas was none too happy with Adam's grin.

They rode well past dark before making camp. Thomas didn't sleep well and woke before the sun had risen. As soon as enough light lit the path he had the men up and moving.

Days turned to a sennight and a sennight to a fortnight and still they found no sign of Penelope. They had talked to so many different clans— Thomas began to think the clans made sport of him. The Scots had sent him and his men on a wild chase that took them many different directions.

He decided that if he didn't find her in another sennight he would send the men back and continue on his own. Though his chances were much better with his men, he couldn't keep them away from Hawkwood forever. He would have to do as Royce said and trust this woman into the Lord's care, for in his heart he knew that she belonged to him. Now if he could have the faith.

†††

Nearly three sennights had passed since

Penelope had left Hawkwood. She missed her friend and she missed Thomas. She even found herself missing the laird as she crept through the forest early that morning, carefully avoiding branches scattered on the ground while swatting away bugs flying around her head. Staying in the shade as much as possible not only kept her from being seen, but the tree shade also afforded a welcome relief from the heat. It was too bad the winged creatures enjoyed cooler air as well.

The woods were alive with the chirping of birds and the chattering of squirrels unhappy to have her in their woods. The beautiful day welcomed as she walked along and for the first time ever she thanked the Lord for the day He had made.

The last time she'd seen Brithwin, her friend's words had touched her, though not at the moment she'd spoken them. But as Penelope had gotten ready for bed that night, it was as if God nudged her just as Brithwin had said He'd done to her. The words weren't audible, but in her heart she knew what she needed to do.

At first she tried to reason why it wasn't a good idea, but then her own words came back to her, and she knew she had to stay true to her promise. Rather than wait until morning, she stole away that night before the portcullis closed.

Voices drew her out of her thoughts and put her on alert. She continued in the direction she needed to go, hoping the voices she heard were going in an opposite direction and would fade. But the more she walked the louder they became until finally she could make out an occasional word. It wasn't another clan as she had thought, but Englishmen on Scottish soil. Silently, she took her bow from her back and pulled an arrow from her quiver, nocking it on the bow.

It would be wise to go around but she needed to know how big of a company they had, for she might be safer to go far down the stream to cross if it was a sizable group spreading out a good bit. As she stole through the trees and underbrush to get a better idea of who she faced, a familiar voice made her stop. Thomas? What was he doing here?

Removing the tension off the nocked arrow, she lowered her bow. Her knees weakened slightly as she then slung the bow back over her shoulder and placed the arrow back in its quiver. She paused to determine if she wanted to step through her cover and into sight. She decided to go with her first plan, and parted the leaves to get a better perspective on what Thomas and his men were doing there.

Thomas stood amongst the men with his back straight and his arms folded. The sun glistened off his wet black hair. He'd probably just bathed in the stream or perhaps dunked his head. He was the tallest one of the group, and though he had ten or more years on the other men with him, he was every bit as fit. She smiled. He and Royce had proved their strength on the practice field many times while she was at Hawkwood.

Her heart hastened, much like before she went into battle. She took a deep breath in an attempt to calm herself. But seeing him standing there, so close, made her miss him all the more. It also made her realize she'd done the right thing…that is if he was as happy to see her as she was to see him.

All the men readied their mounts but Thomas.

Adam, Penelope recognized from when Elfed had challenged her, mounted his destrier as he talked to Thomas. She cocked her head and strained to hear.

"You would be safer if I stayed back with you." Adam said.

"Nay, You go with the others." Thomas replied.

"I do not like it, Thomas. How long will you continue to search?"

Thomas turned and she couldn't hear his response. Indecision tore at her. Before she could change her mind she stepped out of her hiding place.

Adam, up on his horse, spotted her first and nodded her way. "It looks as if the lass has found us."

Chapter 14

Penelope nearly took a step back as Thomas shoved his horse's reins into Adam's hand.

"Hold Wife," he said, and stormed toward her.

"Where have you been?" His already dark-brown eyes went smoldering black.

Penelope lifted her chin and crossed her arms, refusing to be intimidated by the man. "'Tis it not obvious, Thomas?"

"Perhaps I should have asked why did you leave? 'Twas foolish to go off alone." Still angry, he scolded her.

"Weel, you can see I am as capable as you of taking care of myself." She went from happy to see him to as angry at him for being angry at her. This wasn't how she had hoped this reunion would be. "You are lucky I recognized you or you may have found yourself with an arrow in your back."

A grin broke through the frown. "Aye, I am at that. For you would not have missed. Sure I am of that. Now will you tell me why you left Hawkwood with not a word to anyone?"

She was still mad at him for being upset with her. How he could be nearly yelling at her one moment and smiling the next she didn't know.

"I didno' ken I was a prisoner there and had tae give my intentions." She tightened her crossed arms in front of her and glared.

"She's not a good one to make mad, Thomas." One of the men yelled from behind him. "Better give her your peace offering.

"Let us go where there is some privacy." Thomas said as he looked over his shoulder toward the group of men watching them.

They walked down to the stream and sat on a large rock where rushing water pushed up on its side. She loved the water's music as it spilt over and around rocks and the fragrance of wet earth as the water splashed upon the grassy bank.

Thomas pulled one leg up and draped his arm over his knee.

"What is this peace offering your men speak of?" Penelope couldn't imagine what Thomas would bring her.

"I brought you the black. Your spoils from our battle. You earned it. You saved my life."

Penelope couldn't keep the excitement from her voice. "You are giving me the black? 'Tis a beautiful horse. And Royce has agreed?"

"You saved my life, lass."

Guilt struck her. "Aye, but I also almost caused you tae lose it. Dinna think I am unaware that you turned your back because of worry for me."

"'Tis behind us. The beast is yours."

"I thank you, Thomas. 'Tis a beautiful gift."

"And 'tis sorry I am for barking at you when I first saw you, lass. I have been searching this land for over a fortnight. I have had terrible visions of what might have happened to you. 'Twas the fear speaking in anger. I should have trusted fully in the promise I felt God put in my heart. A promise that you were meant for me."

Penelope looked into his dark-brown eyes that seemed to still be smoldering but not with the same emotion. Her stomach lurched. He knew she was meant for him? "You are forgiven. I should have told someone where I headed tae and how long I planned tae be away."

"Be away? You were not leaving Hawkwood?"

"Nay. I planned tae return."

"When we last spoke I said some foolish things. I thought you would never want to see me again."

Penelope opened her mouth to object but Thomas placed his finger on her lips, sending a chill down her body.

"Allow me to say what I need to say."

Penelope nodded, amazed she could feel so much love for a man.

"I never found a woman I thought I could live with when I was younger. I determined I would remain unmarried. But then I met you." He stopped and pushed a wisp of hair behind her ear. "And my heart was feeling things it never had. There you were, a warrior. You could shoot a bow and throw a knife as well as any of men and better than some.

'Twas a hard thing to reconcile myself with, that I had fallen in love with a woman who fought on a battlefield and could hold her own against many of my men.

"And the truth is it scares me to think of you out there fighting beside me. It might very well be the death of me. But I realized if I made you become something you do not want to be then I would be destroying what I love about you. You are who you are and I would not want you any other way."

"Oh, Thomas. I love you." She would tell him later that she had done much thinking, too, and if God were to ever bless them with bairns she would give up her bow and become the mother they would deserve.

He cupped her chin. "Then you will not be marrying any chieftains out of duty. Agreed?"

She smiled. "Nay. I will no' be doing that. 'Tis why I made this trip back here. I took the cross and melted it into twenty-one gold beads, then I went back to my clan and I gave each one of them a gold bead and told them they each had a part of the cross. I told them that it no longer would rule them and they needed it tae find where they belonged. You see, I realized God does no' need a cross tae bless someone. My people had become so fixed on a piece of gold in the shape of a cross they put their faith in it rather than God."

Thomas smiled. "You are a wise lass."

She returned his smile. "I thank you for noticing."

"Oh, lass there is much about you I notice." He

bent his head and met her lips.

Penelope wasn't sure if it was the water rushing down the stream or the pounding of her heart in her ears, but when Thomas's lips met hers, the air grew hotter and the world around her disappeared. The kiss didn't last nearly long enough and when he pulled back, she let out a sigh.

"So will you marry me, lass?" Thomas's stormy eyes seemed to drink her in.

Her heart tripped. She smiled. "I will marry you under one condition."

Penelope almost giggled at the look on Thomas's face.

"And what would that be?" Thomas said the words with hesitation.

"You have tae change your horse's name."

Thomas laughed. "That I can do, lass. That I can do."

If you enjoyed *Sword of the Matchmaker*, you might enjoy the first two novels in the series, *Sword of Forgiveness and Sword of Trust* or another novella from the series, *Sword of the Perfect Bride*.

Debbie Lynne also writes 19th century Charleston, SC stories. If you like southern romance you might like *Shattered Memories and Bride by Blackmail*.

Debbie Lynne Costello is the author of Sword of Forgiveness, Amazon's #1 seller for Historical Christian Romance. She has enjoyed writing stories since she was eight years old. She raised her family and then embarked on her own career of writing the stories that had been begging to be told. She and her husband have four children and live in upstate South Carolina with their 5 horses, 3 dogs, cat and miniature donkey.